biting back
new fiction from the north

editor
Kitty Fitzgerald

David Almond
Andrea Badenoch
Leonard Barras
Chaz Brenchley
Christopher Burns
Fiona Cooper
Julia Darling
Chrissie Glazebrook
Wendy Robertson
Anne Spillard
Michael Standen
Margaret Wilkinson

First published July 2001 by IRON Press
5 Marden Terrace
Cullercoats
North Shields
Northumberland
NE30 4PD
England
Tel/Fax: 0191 253 1901
E-mail: seaboy@freenetname.co.uk

ISBN 0 906228 76 X

Printed by
Peterson Printers, South Shields

© individual authors 2001
typset in Trebuchet MS 9pt

Cover illustrations by Sally Mundy©
Cover and Book Design by
IRON Eye Design @IRON Press

IRON Press books are distributed by
Signature Book Representation Ltd
Sun House, 2 Little Peter St, Manchester M15 4PS
Tel: 0161 834 8767 Fax: 0161 834 8656
E-mail: admin@signature-books.co.uk

Foreword

The motivation behind the publication of this book was the recent upsurge of fiction by writers based in the Northern Arts region of England. The editor of IRON Press, Peter Mortimer, thought it was time to produce a showcase of work by newly published writers like Chrissie Glazebrook and Andrea Badenoch, together with long standing authors such as Wendy Robertson and Christopher Burns. I was delighted when he approached me to edit the collection.

David Almond's first story collections, *Sleepless Nights* and *A Kind of Heaven* were published by IRON Press but it wasn't until the publication of *Skellig* - winner of the Whitbread Prize and the Carnegie Medal - that he achieved international success. Soon after David's breathrough Julia Darling's first novel, *Crocodile Soup* was taken up. She was already well known for her short stories and plays but the publication of her novel propelled her on to the national literary scene and she was long listed for The Orange Prize.

Hot on Julia's heels came Andrea Badenoch with her first crime novel *Mortal*, which was soon followed by *Blink*, both of which achieved critical acclaim. Chrissie Glazebrook's first novel, *The Madolescents*, was then accepted for publication and subsequently became an enormous success. It seemed the right time to celebrate the talent of our regionally based fiction authors.

Not all of the writers we contacted responded to our request to submit stories. Not all the stories which were submitted reached the pages of this book, for a variety of reasons. Peter Mortimer and I read everything which was sent in and this collection is the result of our collaboration. It is not a comprehensive anthology but it does give a taste of the diversity of writing talent based in the region.

The writers were not saddled with a theme or asked to set their work in the north. We wanted to give them the freedom to decide which story they wanted to tell. Nevertheless, **biting back**, does evoke a sense of place and people and begs the question of how far a literary sensibility is formed by its environment, and in turn has an impact on it.

Kitty Fitzgerald
June 2001

Contents

7	*David Almond*	The Built-Up Sole
15	*Andrea Badenoch*	Dog Leg
25	*Leonard Barras*	A Depleted Banjo
33	*Chaz Brenchley*	Beefcake
36	*Christopher Burns*	With
50	*Fiona Cooper*	And Nobody Knew She Was There
62	*Julia Darling*	Geographicals
70	*Chrissie Glazebrook*	The Full Monty
83	*Wendy Robertson*	White Frost on Grass
100	*Anne Spillard*	Tom in a Willow
114	*Michael Standen*	On Double Time
129	*Margaret Wilkinson*	The Intruder
141		*Biographical Notes*

The Built-Up Sole
David Almond

I was watching myself too much in the mirror. Steve dropped his hand across my eyes.

Vanity, he said. Take care. You'll see the devil at your back.

After the darkness, I looked into Felling Square behind. Late afternoon, November. Brilliant autumn light. The older boys were out there, in their bright shirts, their little jackets, their dark glasses.

That's how you could end, he said. Look at them, the nancy boys.

His scissors quickened as the girls strolled past the window, making their way towards the boys. He sucked hard on a cigarette He cursed them all, their bangles and beads, tight jeans, short skirts, their thin-soled pointed shoes. I stared and stared, imagined being out there, until Steve stamped his cigarette out and took his clippers in his fist. I asked if he needed to do this every time and he muttered that it was the only way to get a proper finish. I looked at him: the grubby white tunic buttoned to his throat, the litle pot belly, the bulbous nose. I lowered my head for him. It would soon be over. Soon he'd rub the pink glutinous stuff between his palms, spread it over my scalp, comb it through. It would stiffen in seconds, each hair petrified in place.

Steve was one of those barbers with a built-up sole. The boot on his right foot had a four-inch deep black slab below it. There were many such barbers then.

My mother said that when Steve was a boy disability was commonplace. Men like Steve bore the marks of the old diseases and conditions that now were conquered. A training school in Blyth had taken youths with shortened legs and turned them into barbers. When I complained about the clippers, the slippery pink stuff, Steve's beery breath, she used to say,

Don't be cruel. Think how lucky you are compared with him.

Old men and obedient boys like me were the ones who went to Steve. Boys like those outside the window allowed their hair to grow. They had it trimmed at Crawley's in Low Fell. They went to Gabrielli's in Newcastle and had it washed and styled by Maria or Luigi or Angelo himself.

Time after time I told my mother I was old enough to follow them.

Not yet, she used to say. Steve needs the custom of those like us. Don't be cruel to him, eh? Not yet.

It was Simon who was cruel. And Hutchie, of course. As I lowered my head, there was a tapping at the window. Hutchie. Simon stood over him. He tottered, leaned on the younger boy. He lifted his right foot and showed the thick block of wood tied with string like a roller-skate to his shoe. Steve shoved my head down again, began to dig the clippers into my neck.

These are your friends? he said.

I grunted a reply.

He clippered me again. He brushed the scattered hair out from beneath my collar. He spread the pink stuff on me. He pulled the sheet away from my throat and wiped his hands on it.

Simon lurched back and forward before the window, stepping high then plunging down again.

I handed Steve some coins. He picked some clippings from my collar.

The hairs of your head are numbered, he said. He rested his hand for a moment on my shoulder. You must account for each of them on the day of judgement.

I looked down, yearned to be away from him.

Watch yourself, he said. Take care, now.

He ran his comb for a final time across me, and let me go.

I hurried out to the others: convulsive laughter, convulsive walking to the centre of the square.

At the fountain, I rubbed away the crisp dried dressing. The air was bitter on my temples and neck. Hutchie fingered the stubble there.

Much you pay for that? he said.

I told him and he giggled.

How bloody much?

His own hair was filthy and straight. Jagged bits of it stuck out across his ears. I shoved him away. I borrowed Simon's sole and copied his walk.

I'm Steve, I laughed. Watch out for the nancy boys. Let me stick this pink stuff on your hair.

As dusk came, the older boys and girls gathered on the benches. I'd have her, said Hutchie, peering through the gloom. And her. And her and all.

The streetlights came on. Sergeant Fox strode across the square with his hands behind his back. We stamped our cigarettes out.

Home soon, now, boys, he told us softly.

He nodded towards the others.

Don't follow that lot's ways, not yet.

Steve's window was a great rectangular glare with his name dark upon it. Inside, he swept the floor, he flicked a duster at the mirror.

Wish I was older, I said.

Yes, said Simon. He tipped his head back. The ends of his hair curled across his collar. His breath condensed, rose gently from his face.

Look at her, he whispered.

Her and all, said Hutchie.

I felt my stubble, the icy exposed skin. I imagined hair curling down there, fistfuls of it, hair flopping across my eyes, hair bobbing in the breeze.

Steve took off his white tunic, put a tight-fitting dark coat on. He scooped out the money from his cash drawer. He turned off his lights. He hobbled out, and we laughed at his queer undulating stride.

Let's follow him, said Hutchie.

Leave him alone, I said.

Ha! said Hutchie.

Simon flung his mock sole into a flower bed and led us away. We waited in doorways while Steve called at The Blue Bell's off licence and at Todd's newsagents.

We followed him through the dim yellow light of the streetlights, the icy mist, the shadows beyond the High Street towards his bedsit in the new blocks where the terraces had been. In front of us was the clink of his bottles, the slap of his heavy boot, the click of his light one.

We hesitated on some waste ground.

Simon touched my temple and smiled.

You want to come with us? he said.

I nodded. I held his hair for a second between my fingers.

You don't know what we'll be up to, he said.

I'll come, I said.

Hutchie laughed.

I'll come, he mocked.

Come on, then, he said. He'll be inside by now.

We moved again. Steve's light came on. He

came to his window, tugged his curtains together. I stayed close to Simon while Hutchie hurried on.

Why do you let him come with you? I said.

Simon shrugged.

You wouldn't do what he'll do, he said.

He held the back of my neck and stared into my eyes.

You wouldn't, he said. Would you?

There were lights in the windows of the other blocks, but the curtains were closed, and no one would be able to see out into the night.

Hutchie looked into Steve's window through the tunnel of his hands.

All alone, he told us. Poor little soul.

He grinned.

When I was little I used to be scared of him, he said.

He turned his face towards the bedsit.

Cripple, he whispered. Cripple.

Tell him, said Simon.

Cripple. Cripple.

He held his laughter in.

Let's get him back, said Simon.

Aye. Teach him a lesson he won't forget.

They grinned at each other.

Coming? said Simon, touching me again. Ha. Not you.

Hutchie giggled.

Much did you say you paid for that?

They went to the entrance to the block.

I went to the window and peered in. There was a narrow gap where the curtains didn't meet.

Steve was in his chair. There was a bottle of beer and a glass on a table before him. He was reading a magazine from Todd's. A long-legged girl on the cover stood on tiptoe in the sea. Her breasts were outlined against the sky. Steve's discarded boots were on the floor. His shortened leg was curled beside him. I saw his little white foot, his stunted toes. He raised his head, listened, stood up and lurched to his door. Hutchie came in first. Then Simon kicked the door closed and held Steve from behind and kept his hand across Steve's eyes. He whispered into Steve's ear. I closed my eyes and when I opened them again Hutchie was at the glass, his face level with mine. He opened the curtains inches wider, letting me see everything that he did inside.

Nothing much, just simple things. He smashed the beer bottle on the wall. He upended the table. He ripped Steve's magazine into little pieces and scattered them on the floor. He pulled Steve's built-up boot on. He bared his teeth at Steve. He spat at him. He dug his finger into Steve's cheek and whispered what must have been curses and warnings at him. He shoved his hand down into Steve's pocket and took out some coins. Steve didn't struggle. He just hung loosely in Simon's arms until he was allowed to fall, and lay there until the boys went out again into the night.

As they came past me, Hutchie shoved the coins into my hand. It cost you nowt, he said. Hutchie leaned on Simon and they giggled as they hobbled into the night. I waited by the window. At last Steve pulled the curtains aside and looked out through his hands. No way of knowing if he saw me there, or if he knew me. Tears trickled through his fingers onto the glass. I headed back through the darkness towards the square. I made my way through the older girls and boys. Sergeant Fox was at the fountain as I passed. He muttered it was time for home now, wasn't it?

I kept Steve's money in a little dish in my bedroom. For some time I was thought of as rebellious. I refused to have my hair cut. I said I'd grown beyond all that. My mother asked me to think of poor Steve, but soon she started to say it was maybe time to go to Crawley's. I wouldn't go. I loved to feel my hair between my fingers, to tug it down towards my collar.

Simon and Hutchie were breaking up. Simon wore a leather jacket and dark glasses. He grew taller, more languid, his hair hung in exquisite waves around his face. He spent time with the girls in the square. He turned away if I passed by. Hutchie wandered twitchily on his own, or picked up younger kids to walk with him. His hair bushed out, spiky and uncontrollable. I never met his eye.

If I looked towards Steve's shop, I saw the limping man in the white tunic, the wall of mirrors, the old men and the boys. Nothing seemed to have changed.

It was almost Christmas when we heard that Steve had gone mad. He'd been drinking in The Blue Bell. He'd gone out into the dark, hobbled across the square to his shop. He kicked the window in with his built-up boot. He climbed inside and smashed the mirrors. He started to tear his shops to bits. By the time Sergeant Fox climbed in to him he was lying on the floor in a litter of scissors and clippers and broken glass. He was bleeding, foaming at the mouth, gurgling, howling. The policeman held him down. He called to the watching crowd to get some reinforcements.

Next day, the broken glass had been cleared from the pavement, but the shop was full of debris. You could see patches of dried blood. A few boards were nailed where the window had been. Hair cuttings blew out through the gaps. Sergeant Fox stood by the door. There was a great white bandage on his right hand and an elastoplast on his cheek. He warned us to keep back for our own protection.

Yes, he said. The human mind is indeed a mysterious thing.

As I walked back across the square, Hutchie was with a bunch of little kids. He had Steve's built-up boot on. He was hobbling in circles, grunting, going mad.

I'm Steve, he said. I'm bloody Steve.

I was there, he said when he saw me. He was wild.

Take it off, I said.

I held him by the throat, made him take it off and give it to me.

Simon was watching, and he smiled at me.

Your hair, he said as I passed by. It's coming on.

The boot dangled from my hand as I left the square. I felt the sullen stubborn weight of its built-up sole. I saw that there was nothing I could do, and I flung it into the piles of rubble where the terraces had been.

We heard that Steve had been taken to Prudhoe. My mother said we should visit him there, take some Christmas cake and sherry for him. She said she'd heard that his shop was to be sold. There were rumours that Crawley intended to take over.

Will you go back then? she asked.

I shrugged.

She clicked her tongue and pulled my hair.

This mess, she said. You must sort it out before Christmas.

On Saturday, I emptied the dish of Steve's money. I went on the bus to Newcastle. I sat in the line of gleaming chairs in Gabrielli's. My hair was washed in warm water by Maria. It was trimmed and styled and left to curl over my collar by the gentle hands of Angelo himself.

Dog Leg
Andrea Badenoch

It's hard to recognise the landscape now, but until the summer when Shelley-Ann turned fourteen, Dog Leg was a warren of old streets, a collection of tottering tenements and dark cobbled lanes. After that summer, of course, everything changed, but some still remember how it was before the marina came, and the swanky hotels, before all the yak-yak about urban renewal, the sculpture park, pricey restaurants and young students on unicycles doing street theatre. As strange as it might seem more than a decade on, people used to actually *live* on Dog Leg, marooned within its tight triangle of river, railway and canal. It was their home.

Shelley-Ann was the youngest in her family, and the slowest with her harelip and squinty stare. She never learned to read and write and one day simply refused to go to school. "No more school," she declared.

Every day there'd be an argument. "Get ready and go to school!" But she wouldn't. Even though she'd plenty of friends, they'd always treated her as if she were special, as if she were a baby. They'd made gentle fun of her slowness. So Shelley-Ann began avoiding the boys and girls she'd grown up with. She started going her own way, doing her own thing. Nobody could stop her. She wasn't listening. She wasn't even hearing.

Shelley-Ann started getting up late and dressing carefully. She wore a nylon sleeveless top and she stuffed tissues in her brassiere to emphasise her girlish breasts. She wore a ragged pair of denim shorts an ankle chain and rope-soled cheaply fashioned shoes. She pulled her thin fair hair into a flag on the top of her head and outlined her eyes with blue crayon. She tinted her lips pearly-pink. Shelley-Ann's rabbity, twisted face could never be pretty, but what she did was make herself look available. Despite everything, despite all her disadvantages, she possessed a unique and peculiar sexual allure.

A few families, including Shelley-Ann's, had lived on Dog Leg for a hundred and fifty years. They were a separate community in the heart of the city. They spoke their own dialect, kept their own rules and harmed no-one. They were all related, handing down their used clothing, breathing each other's air. They crowded into narrow rooms with primitive sanitation and paper-thin partitions. They strung their washing across alleys and worked hard. In the evenings they sat on their steps, gossiping and drinking tea. They took care of their children and were wary of strangers.

That last summer, just after Shelley-Ann turned fourteen, the weather was hot and unrelenting. The sun jabbed between the high and ancient buildings of Dog Leg, the sky a narrow, cloudless strip. The canal and river started to smell, and without the benefit of rain, refuse and dogshit collected in gutters. People breathed the dry and dusty air, listening to the sound of machinery not far away. They were both nervous and enervated in the exceptional heat, poised on the brink of change because bulldozers were coming and there was nothing they could do to stop them. All avenues of protest were closed. Dog Leg was being demolished.

Shelley-Ann was in a world of her own. She wore a pair of tiny headphones and with her eyes closed, lying on the sofa, she sang along to the lyrics of pop songs as if they had special meaning. "Like a virgin," she crooned, "touched for the very first time ..." Her toe nails were painted black. She adopted a teetering, sleazy walk which made her seem both vulnerable and knowing. She watched a lot of television and every so often she would disappear outside, swinging her plastic, see-through shoulder bag, meeting but not meeting the eyes of passers by with her curiously off-centre gaze, her misshapen lips pouting. She never said where she was going. She went in the direction of the crashing masonry, the virile shouts on the new and ever changing edge of things.

Dog Leg was being flattened. The City Fathers had succumbed to its *potential*. In other words a developer had made them an offer they couldn't refuse and pockets were being lined. Railway sheds and grimy old car showrooms were already tumbling along the limits of the boundaries with uneasy groans. The batter-batter of the ball on the crane thumped throughout daylight hours and above it brick dust tried to eclipse the sun. Fires were lit. There were hell-like plumes of sulphur and other smouldering chemicals and the big diggers kept on roaring. Men in plastic hats yelled instructions to lorry drivers, their faces blackened with dirt and sweat. Each day these contracted destroyers drew nearer and nearer to people's homes. There was no relief. Even the short, anxious nights were eerily menacing with the smell of engine oil carried on the river's midnight breeze. Dog Leg was shrinking, disappearing, falling down. The families were under siege, as if living near the epicentre of an unstoppable war.

"Where's our Shelley-Ann gone?" someone would ask in a way that was both worried and not worried. "Our Shelley-Ann's gone down among those workmen." Women fanned themselves with newsprint without reading the news. "That Shelley-Ann's up to no good." They both knew and didn't want to know the truth. "She's alright, I think. Isn't she? Isn't she?" They shook their heads, shrugged their shoulders. After a while no one even tried to dissuade her. Shelley-Ann kept disappearing, that was all. People leaned in doorways, not behaving like themselves. The atmosphere was both electrically charged and disablingly static in alternate waves. Both everything and nothing seemed possible and normal rules no longer had meaning. Shelley-Ann's rebellion was at once shocking and mundane.

One night, very late, there was shouting and the patter of footsteps and then a frantic knocking on doors along the row. Curtains were pulled back and several residents stepped blearily into the muggy darkness. Shelley-Ann stood under a street lamp, her hair down, her face smeared with tears, her legs muddy and grazed. She still carried her bag but her t-shirt was torn from the neck almost to her waist. She was out of control, sobbing strange words. Her shorts were undone. She kicked the kerb, hit her own chest with her fists and swore obscenely in a way that was unknown on Dog Leg.

"No, no, no!" she shrieked as her auntie and girl cousins led her inside. "I never said I wanted to!"

"Sshh, sshh, quieten down," they murmured, wrapping her in a blanket, handing her a cup of warmed milk. "Sshh, little one, it's OK, it's safe now." They laid her in an armchair whilst in the hallway an uncle's hand reached for the telephone.

"Not that," whispered the cousins in unison, "leave her be, for now." They stroked her brow and hands and smoothed her hair. Her cheek was bruised, her expression pinched and wary. They noticed how her misaligned features were blotched, sullied and curiously older. Her mother came and then her sisters and grandmother. They all sat around her in a protective female wall, their backs hunched against the inexplicable world outside. Beyond them, through the thin curtains, the sun rose determinedly above the ruined skyline, its rays as solid and rich as blood. Shelley-Ann became quiet at last but her fists were clenched. She wasn't calm.

"I'm a dead person," she said unaccountably, her eyes staring. "I'm a dead person, floating in The Nib." She gulped her milk. She told a curious tale which seemed to make no sense. Her voice was tentative, uncertain. She said that she got lost in the dark down by the canal where all the familiar landmarks had disappeared. There was a new high mesh fence, a mountain of rubble that only recently had been the tannery and beyond this a series of portokabins she had never seen before. Some heavy vehicles were idle and grouped together. It was black with no stars and she thought she saw a figure ahead of her in the gloom. "It seemed like a lady or maybe a boy. I couldn't see clearly. I called out, to ask which way to go but they looked at me and ran away." Her family listened attentively. She sat upright, slipped off her blanket and hugged her knees to her chest. "I followed. I thought if I keep this person ahead of me, then in the end I'll get back to our house." She described how she had to hurry because they were almost running.

"Who was it?" asked her auntie.
Shelley-Ann shook her head. She said they were wearing shorts or a short skirt and that all she could make out was the whiteness of their arms flashing in the shadows. "We seemed to be going towards the river, but everything was different and I couldn't be sure." She said she passed a tall brick building with broken windows and a crane growing out of the roof. "It might have been Delaney's." She said she crossed a new metal bridge where piles of bricks were stacked above her head like a wall. There were no pavements left, no proper roads. "The multistorey's gone. Even the swings are gone. And where's the old church?" She looked perplexed. The

ground under her feet had been churned to dust with the deep imprints of tyres. The cobbles were uprooted. "I couldn't catch them up. I thought it might be Jackie Rockingham's brother. The little one. Or Mrs Maguire. I speeded up but they were always ahead of me. Then I got to The Nib."

The Nib was a thin channel which linked the canal to the river with a lock at either end. It was deep and its Victorian structure was stained with black and green slime. It was permanently overcast by windowless bonded warehouses. It was seldom used even before all the changes. Refuse coagulated on its oily surface. It was a dark, unwelcoming place.

"You've been told to stay away from there," her mother whispered, almost to herself.

"I looked down," muttered Shelley-Ann, her voice barely audible. "But the person had gone. There was only a body." At this point she started to cry again and her white fists drummed on the arms of her chair. She started swaying and her sobs became rhythmic, hysterical, inconsolable. One of her sisters noticed a bite mark above her left breast. Her uncle and boy cousins appeared, looked at each other wordlessly, then set off in the direction of The Nib. Her auntie forced brandy with hot lemonade into her mouth.

"You don't understand," she said eventually. "That dead body. It wasn't Mrs Maguire. It wasn't Joey Rockingham. I saw it clear as anything. It was floating face up. It was *me*."

A few days passed. Nothing was found in The Nib except a carrier bag of drowned kittens and a rusted pushchair. Shelley-Ann was made to stay in bed and her old friends came round and gave her comics and a bag of sticky sweets. She couldn't remember getting home, couldn't explain her injuries, her torn clothing. A group of men were chosen to go and speak to the foreman of the contractors but still nothing became clear. He said, "That girl who hangs about here? She's fucking daft. None of my men have touched her." But no one really doubted that something bad had happened to Shelley-Ann, something that had frightened her terribly, made her see things. But they didn't tell the police. This wasn't their way.

Shelley-Ann herself was unable to recount more than she'd already offered. She began changing the subject when questioned. The issue was uneasily dropped and the curious lethargy of the previous weeks re-established. The sun continued to beat down on the altering landscape. The earth movers churned inwards, their massive wheels slow but emotionless. Dog Leg families started to load their possessions into vans, their reluctant destination an unlovable council highrise north of the bus station. This was on the other side of town. Meanwhile their grocer's shop closed, then their betting shop, then their Chinese takeaway. The very first homes began to crash to the ground in pieces and others were torn open revealing sad floral wallpaper, abandoned wardrobes, pathetic possessions such as chipped enamel bowls. Odd items stood in what had been the street - an empty bird cage on a stand, a toddler's pedal car, an ironing board. People stopped, stared then walked away. "The Longs lived there," said a man, gesturing feebly a broken fireplace. "The Longs were born and died there." His words hung unheard in the hot, still air until the bulldozers resumed their roaring.

Shelley-Ann's family were not the last to leave but they were among the last. They smoothed out their letters from the housing authority and put them neatly under the fruit bowl, but for a long while refused to read them. In the end they saw they were to be split up and scattered. The highrise had become full so Shelley-Ann's grandmother was allocated a flat near the abattoir across the river. Most were offered a suburb miles away. Some of the cousins were told to report to a bed and breakfast hotel near the airport. Finally, they all began packing. They did this in a resigned way without speaking. They were neither excited nor bitter. They wrapped their best china in newspaper and carefully folded their clothes.

On the last morning before the transits arrived, there was no sign of Shelley-Ann. "Where's that girl?" asked her mother. She sighed. "Where's she got to now?" A few hours passed. As the sky turned scarlet and the eerie evening quiet descended on Dog Leg the van doors were squeezed together and tied with rope. "We can't go without her."

They paired off to begin an organised search. "That Shelley-Ann's stupid," said a cousin, impassively. No one argued, but it was the first time one of them had ever said such a thing. Two of her brothers went down to the canal. The water was unusually low and there was a fetid smell. They paused, trying to get their bearings. The view of the city beyond Dog Leg was new. Everything was opened up. Glassy office blocks reflected the red sky and the modern ring road curved away on stilts. "The old tannery was here," said one, gesturing to an empty space where the rubble had recently been cleared. They paused. There was a high mesh fence which seemed to be guarding nothing. They walked towards a group of portokabins which were shut up for the night. Their doors were padlocked and barred. Next to them, heavy vehicles were immobilised. Their massive tyres were caked with Dog Leg's earth, their bodies garish yellow and blue.

"She's not here. Let's go down to the river." They followed a broad track which had been created by the contractors. It was a deep rut and didn't correspond to the old pattern of streets. They were disoriented but could make out the line of the canal's towpath in the fading light.

"It's this way."

"Is it?"

"Yeah."

They walked for a while. They passed a tall, once handsome building whose windows were broken and whose doors were torn from their hinges. Behind, a crane stood to attention, illuminated by little lights. The cousins stopped.

"Delaney's," one said, without feeling.

"You remember I used to work here?" was the reply, "When I first left school? It's where I met Carol."

"Looks a bit of a state now."

"He got compensation. Old man Delaney. Not like the rest of us."

"Yeah, well he's in on it, isn't he?"

"Come on."

They crossed a new metal bridge over the canal which had been created for the builders' delivery lorries. Piles of bricks towered above them, some still on pallets, half wrapped in polythene. They picked their way through the ruins of the multistorey carpark and then climbed over a low wall that had once been the edge of a children's playground. The swings and roundabouts had gone leaving gashes in the soft tarmac safety surface. They could see the bank of the river, its greenish edge revealed, and a few toppling gravestones next to where there had been a church. They turned their eyes away from a board, lying in the dirt, which still ornately bore the numbers of hymns. In the distance, The Nib's bonded warehouses were three quarters demolished. They walked slowly towards the deep channel that had been more or less disused for years. They took deep breaths. It still smelt the same - stagnant, sweetish, oily. They remembered it from their childhoods. It was a place they'd always been instructed not to go, although sometimes, out of bravado they'd swung on the rusty guard rails above the locks, dropping in stones, before running away, scared. There were king rats, so they'd been told, infections, bad men. The black water was fathomless and filthy. It was now easier to reach The Nib's brick edge. A broad swathe had been created with rubble piled on either side. The daylight had almost gone but an incongruous streetlight remained standing casting a yellow pool. They hesitated. Even now, the place retained its terrors. They clutched each other's hands like boys and moved forwards. They leaned over and looked down into the depths. One of them muffled a scream.

Shelley-Ann was clearly visible. She was half floating, half wedged against the metal gate of a lock. Her body was naked, white and slightly twisted like a redundant mannequin dummy. The side of her head was caved in. Even from where they were standing they could make out her painted toe nails, her smudged lipstick and attached to nothing, but wound around her neck, the wire from her little headphones, one of which was still in her ear.

A Depleted Banjo
Leonard Barras

Was Jonathan Carver wrong to adopt an elephant? Was it his answer to his wife's hamster-fancying? He was a reticent man and felt he owed no explanations to the world, least of all to his father-in-law, who would only have quoted Wells or Plutarch.

"H.G. Wells," the old man told him, "once said that we must find heroic enterprises for the young." It was Saturday, their day for meeting on the stairs.

"It's been a mild winter up to now," Carver stated. This was as much expansion as he permitted himself.

His father-in-law said "H'm," and laboured up the stairs to sit on the landing, trying to remember the words of *Keep Right On To The End Of The Road*, while Carver proceeded to the living room, where the elephant met him with an unsure eye. Timothy was an elephant with feelings of inadequacy. This was because Beryl Carver declined to transfer her affections from the hamsters, arguing that in the event of an invasion by Jutes an elephant was constitutionally ill-equipped to fly off with a message for help.

"So are hamsters!" Carver accused.

"You are thinking of pigeons!" Beryl asserted.

They both were, but were equal in their senselessness to justice.

Beryl's father, P.V. Shackleton, was well aware that it had been a mild winter. People at the bus stop kept saying they wished it would turn cold to kill off the germs. His response was that if he had ever felt as bitterly as that about germs he would have gone and sat in the deep freeze of Percy Crowe, the all-night butcher. In any case, scientists, not that he trusted them, averred that the human frame could not stand up to total purity. A germ-free atmosphere, like neat whisky, was a guaranteed recipe for making your quietus.

At the bus stop, he talked about Plutarch, scientists and the day he was kicked in the leg, unless the man in the deerstalker hat and the woman with the shopping trolley were not there, coughing, in which case he tried to remember the words of *Roamin' in the Gloamin'*. On the whole, he would have preferred not to hang about bus stops in mild weather, but at home there was nothing but the recriminations of his daughter and son-in-law drifting up the stairs.

He had first been attracted to the works of Sir Harry Lauder when, as a child, he had heard that Scots bard singing at the Empire Theatre, slightly ahead of the orchestra. Thirty years later, he had said to his fiancée, "I shall always think of you as Mary, ma Scots bluebell." His fiancée, an expatriate cockles and mussels vendor named Molly Malone, was hoping to go to the cinema, but P.V. Shackleton had already settled at his banjo to accompany his own rendering, minus most of the lyric, of *I Love a Lassie*.

"Are you sure we're well-matched?" his fiancée asked. It was her wish to see Bing Crosby in *Ben Hur*.

"Are you sitting on my string?" he enquired. His banjo string kept falling off.

Another fifty years on, he was still singing Harry Lauder's ill-remembered lyrics to his depleted banjo, while his daughter and son-in-law sat downstairs, upbraiding each other over the elephant.

It was undeniable, Jonathan Carver conceded, that they had no pigeons, but after much thought he rejoined, "By converse reasoning, no elephant in full flight is likely to dash himself to pieces against a lighthouse."

After much thought, Beryl rejoined, " Neither would hamsters."

These mutual reproaches had their effect on Timothy, and soon his sense of inadequacy was hopelessly entrenched. Carver was a failed footballer and he compensated by teaching the reluctant elephant goalkeeping, while Beryl, driven by her fear that the Jutish hordes would descend, wrote feverish letters to MIs 5 and 6, denouncing their gas suppliers, Hengist & Horsa PLC, as Anglo-Saxon infiltrators. MIs 5 and 6 suspected this, but were not telling each other. When she had been no more than three-and-a-half, her father had sung to her Harry Lauder's *Will You Stop Your Ticklin', Jock?* slightly ahead of his banjo, so clearly the old man bore some responsibility for her xenophobia.

One night it rained, cutting short the goalkeeping, and Carver and the elephant hurried indoors, where the elephant shook himself, extinguishing the TV set and severing Beryl from civilisation.

" You think you can re-live your failed youth through that elephant" , she shouted. " Another thing - this very afternoon, I heard the bagpipes in the distance!" She believed that Jutes played bagpipes as an encore to pillaging. In fact, it was *'It's Nice to Get Up in the Mornin'*, being played in the bathroom on a depleted banjo.

" Beryl," Carver said doggedly, " this elephant did not ask to be born. I cannot forget Wells's dictum that we must find heroic enterprises for the young."

" I said it first!" P.V. Shackleton contradicted from the landing.

Beryl was not, it should be made partially plain, the daughter of the fiancée whom P.V. Shackleton had courted half-a-century earlier, for that lady did not become his wife. She could not live up to his requirement:" Love me, love my banjo."

" I wanted to see Bing Crosby," she objected, breaking off their engagement. She learned too late - but still unreliably - that Bing Crosby had been supplanted by Harpo Marx, although that knowledge would hardly have prevailed with a banjoist. " My destiny hung on a string," she told her best friend.

" Was it not Sydney Greenstreet?" asked her archetypal best friend, well-meaning but useless, and making the least of her scanty appearance in this fable.

Shackleton married on the rebound the girl who was to become his daughter's mother. From that marriage there would spring his dislike of Southend-on-Sea. If Sydney Greenstreet had starred in *Ben Hur*, would the whole face of the earth have changed? Would Shackleton still have become the old man who rode daily six times on the 325 circular bus?

Only that morning, he had asked people at the bus stop if they had any thoughts on germs or the Philosopher's Stone, or for that matter, Plutarch's aphorisms. Most of them were coughing at the time. " Plutarch," Shackleton said, " claimed that at forty every man is a fool or his own physician. So much for germs."

" Which bus do you get?" the man enquired.

" There have always been germs," said Shackleton, " and unless they talk about me behind my back or take my place in the bus queue, I'm inclined to say: Live and let live."

" I think this is your bus," the man said.

" Well, no," Shackleton explained. " I get the 325."

" It'll do for me," the man said.

" I'm sure that man's got on the wrong bus,"

Shackleton told the woman with the shopping trolley. "Did you notice his cough?"

" I think this is my bus," the woman said.

He had been going to tell her about Percy Crowe's father, who had the worst cough in six counties. " You should do something about that cough," people said to him (scientists mostly). He would have told her Percy's father's reply, if he could have remembered it, but she was dragging her shopping trolley on to a bus.

" I would come with you," he called after her, "but I have to go home." In any case, the foolish woman was also on the wrong bus. It was Saturday and his son-in-law was due to meet him on the stairs to say " Is it still raining?" or " I see the wind's dropped," his weekly gesture to communication.

Jonathan Carver's greetings were growing ever more perfunctory. He was beginning to reflect that Wells, brilliant theorist though he might have been, had never faced the practicality of an elephant in his daily life. Not Beatrice Webb nor the entire Fabian Society had the answer to that.

" Will somebody post these letters?" Beryl Carver asked, having scribbled another thirteen. Letters were piling up at MIs 5 and 6 and extra staff were being taken on to ignore them.

" How is the mole on your shoulder?" Carver enquired. He was scarcely interested in the mole on his wife's shoulder, but it was another of his gestures to communication.

Beryl had gone to the airing cupboard to feed the hamsters. " Did you know," she demanded, " that we're out of pease pudding?"

" Unhappiness is a by-product," P.V. Shackleton shouted downstairs. He was an authority on unhappiness and had shouted downstairs for many years, regarding it as the right of every husband and father-in-law. His wife, Beryl's mother, had borne this as long as possible, but had eventually kicked him in the leg and gone to Southend-on-Sea.

It was raining again and Carver, oppressed by the prospect of a damp elephant about the house following the nightly goalkeeping, took the steaming beast aside and pressed a twenty-pound note into his trunk.

"Timothy," he said, avoiding the reproachful eyes, "I want you to slip around to the all-night butcher's to fetch a bag of pease pudding for the hamsters. And while you're about it, post these three hundred damned letters."

The elephant pulled on his galoshes and went forlornly out into the rain.

On the landing, P.V. Shackleton intoned "Awa' in the valley, the pibroch is sounding ..." to his banjo. It was as much as he could remember of Sir Harry Lauder's *Hame o' Mine*. Well, compromise was another by-product, he knew, and it was in the search for the Philosopher's Stone that Bötticher had hit on Dresden china. He would mention that at the bus stop on Monday.

He would also tell the woman with the shopping trolley what Percy Crowe's father had said to the scientists. "There are people in the cemetery," he had said, "who wish they had a cough like this." That was what he had said to scientists, coughing in their faces, and he had lived to be 89 and died friendless.

The night wore on. Timothy did not return. In a silence broken only by the hamsters as they called crossly for their pease pudding, the Carvers sat, enveloped in mutual guilt, both wondering if their selfishness had alienated the innocent elephant of their marriage.

It was midnight when the battering came at the

door.

" There's a battering," P.V. Shackleton shouted down. " At the door."

But Beryl had hurtled upstairs past him to put on her nightie, believing that Hengist and Horsa had arrived to murder her in her bed. She was resigned to meeting them halfway, like all condemned persons who connive at their own execution.

Carver answered the knock. The elephant was on the step, leaning heavily against a policeman.

" Do you identify this pachyderm?" the officer asked.

Carver said it was self-evident, citing the mole on his wife's shoulder.

" Is that material and relevant?" asked the policeman.

" I mention it," Carver admitted, " only because I have always thought it a dull place to have a mole."

At that, Beryl rushed downstairs. " Take me, Saxon avenger," she cried, " but spare this elephant!"

" She thinks you're a gasman," Carver explained.

The policeman said it was a common error among the laity. " It has come to our notice," he pursued, " that the elephant in question, being in possession of a twenty-pound note, acquired a bottle of spirits. He then proceeded to the premises of Percy Crowe, all-night butcher, shutting himself in the cold room."

" Oh, what have you done, Timothy?" Carver moaned.

" Where is the pease pudding?" asked Beryl.

" I cannot vouch for his state of mind," said the policeman, " but the evidence is that he had some thought of sitting in the deep freeze, in a germ-proof atmosphere, drinking neat whisky, with a view to making his quietus."

" Damn Southend-on-Sea!" P.V. Shackleton shouted from the landing.

" By all means, sir," said the policeman, " if it's not too late. Goodnight, madam. Goodnight, gentlemen."

Jonathan and Beryl Carver carried Timothy upstairs, past the old man, laid him on his bed and went back to the living room to recriminate

In a while, P.V. Shackleton entered Timothy's room. They gazed at each other, old man and young elephant. The old man would have sung Harry Lauder's *Keep Right On To The End Of The Road*, if only he could have remembered the words. " Tell you what," he said at last. " On Monday, I'll take you on the 325 bus."

Beefcake
Chaz Brenchley

Since he began his visits, her skin had grown paper-thin; countless clumsy encounters with the kitchen table or the bedstead had left her legs a mottled mass of red and purple.

" Look at me," her reed-voice whispered, while her reedy fingers gestured weakly. " Like a well-marbled slab of prime Northumbrian beef ..."

She was always fond of irony. These days she lived on egg custard and high-protein drinks, slops she called them, all that her stomach could tolerate.

Paper-thin her skin, and folded like crêpe paper, testament to a long survival. When she dressed, when she could bear the weight of clothes against her bones, she dressed like Edith Sitwell in her age. Even now, lying on her bed wearing nothing but an antique silk kimono, she insisted on adornment. A great chain of gold and rubies at her throat, pinching jaundiced chicken-flesh and jutting from the harsh rims of her collarbones, bruising everywhere it touched; rings on every finger, rings of onyx and garnet and cornelian, too grossly sized for taste or sense. She could hardly move her trembling hands for the sheer brutal mass of them. Even the livid varnish on her nails might have proved too much for her, but she would have it all, and so she did. What else was he there for, but to give her the world, or as much - or as little - of it as she could handle?

" I try to keep the world away," she said, reading his thought, misunderstanding. " I do try, I do ..."

He knew that, all too well. Who better? She rarely left her bedroom, never her flat. But the world out there was in here also, all her life was in here and she fitted it as poorly as she fitted her clothes now. Typically - yearning always for what was impossible, what was utterly gone - he wished he'd known her forty years before, when she was young and outrageous. Too late: it was the accumulation of all those years that outraged here, time and sickness and the cruel physicality of things that would not soften or fray to match her softened, fraying body in these last days.

" I abdicated," she said, " but I was a queen, and they will not let me go ..."

That was true, *but neither she them* was the whole truth of it. He wished he could be a boy in history, in her history, a figure in the photographs that sheened the walls with glamour. That was his tragedy, to serve her in her decay when all he wanted was to have thrown himself at her feet when she could still wear spikes and spike men on them. To have thrown himself down and been picked up, that was implicit: to have been kissed and mocked, named and accepted, one among the entourage. No more than that.

Not possible. He was all the entourage she had. Once she commanded dozens, with a flick of her stately head; now there was him and only him. He came daily, but she never let him stay. An hour's cooking, an hour's cleaning, an hour to help her in the bathroom: nothing more than that, and that was nothing to what he wanted. He wanted to take her out, to parade her, to show her ghosts of herself in the gleaming streets and have her murmur " Pale imitations," as they were. He thought she should bathe in remembered glory, he thought she should suffer the admiration of the world, but she would not.

Like her, he found the world too solid, too apt

to bruise. He longed for flight, for displacement, to dance with harmless shadows to the known rhythm of a repeated song; she retreated, further and further from anything that threatened. The day would come, he knew, when she would not leave her bed at all; but even then, he thought the weight of her duvet would bruise her bones while the bed-springs dug at her back.

Well, he wanted to cry, like a man too late at a party, *let's have that again, from the top now, there's room for a little one more*; instead he said, " Well, what more can I do for you today?"

" Shave me," she said, lifting a straining hand to rub her fingers' tips against the loose soft skin of her cheek.

" I did that already."

" Again, do it again," she said fretfully, rubbing and rubbing, rubbing through the foundation he'd so painstakingly applied at her direction. The sleeve of her kimono fell away, to show a faded tattoo on her shrunken arm.

The reality of her body was a thing that neither of them could escape, although they tried loyally, each for the other's sake.

" Stubble," she said, " I can feel stubble. I never did have hairs on my chest, I was always lucky there, even when I was beefcake," and she pulled open the kimono to show him her luck, though he knew it all already: the fallen ribs and the inverted nipples and no, no hair at all except between her legs where her cock lay nested and flaccid and all but forgotten, no luck there. " Behold, my brother Esau is a hairy man, but I am a smooth man," she said." Shave me again."

New Fiction from the North

With
Christopher Burns

The new commander's confidence and glory were short-lived. In October 1652 his fleet was routed and forced to flee for refuge behind sandbanks off the Dutch coast. All of Witte de With's ambition, all of his dreams had come to nothing. Who knows the despair and forlorn hopes that must have filled his mind in those terrible hours, as his ambition skulked with his vessels in those shallow waters?

- Stoop: *A History of the Netherlands.*

The barge was painted a green that was as dark and shiny as the green of holly leaves, and its varnished interior was as close as any refuge. Bobby and I saw it by one of those chances that are so fragile that later they seem to be the fulfilment of a destiny.

I had known Bobby for only six weeks before we became lovers. Our affair deepened in a series of hurried assignations lasting little more than half an hour, sometimes less. The passion we felt for each other was so ferocious that we had no time for guilt, or to consider that what we were doing was wrong. Nevertheless it took weeks of scheming and lies before we could arrange a stolen night together. Bobby told his wife, and I told my husband, that we were being sent to a conference. It was a believable lie; we had each attended them before. We didn't want to go, we elaborated, but we'd been given no choice.

Our excitement was sharpened by the drabness of the lives he and I lived while we were apart. As soon as we were in the hotel room he locked the door and we made love on the floor. I remember that I rested one of my outstretched legs on the side of the bed, and that my tights, which Bobby thought he had removed, slithered little by little down the calf of one leg from where they had bunched around the ankle.

Afterwards we celebrated the talents that had brought us together. Bobby and I shared an ambition, and because this had always been frustrated, we believed it to be a passion. Conversations about art had brought us together; now, in a silence broken only by the faint scratch of pencil on paper, we each sketched the other's portrait. We told each other how good we were and how shameful it would be to allow such gifts to wither. When we had finished we each studied the other's idealised image of our features. It was easy to agree that there were painters who made a comfortable living from their work, and that many of them were far less accomplished than us.

That night we slept little. We laughed a lot, and could not bear not to be touching the other's body, but when we talked about the next day, we both fell silent.

In the morning our love seemed hopeless and bittersweet. Lost opportunities smothering our thoughts, we breakfasted beside French windows overlooking a river fished by a solitary angler.

Later I sat quietly in Bobby's car as he drove back towards the motorway and the suburbs, his wife, my husband, his children, mine.

We understood each other's silence. It was absurd that we should return to such places, and to people we had outgrown. We were special. We were different. Why should we be tied to the everyday?

Bobby drove over a trellis bridge which we must have driven across the day before and not even noticed. Now we looked down through the green metal struts and saw a boatyard with moored barges. Perhaps a plan of escape began to form at that moment.

Bobby suggested that we stop for ten minutes and pulled up onto a gravel park alongside the canal. We walked beside the barges hand-in-hand like newly-weds. Their colours were bright and sharp, green, red, and black; gambling colours. Beyond the barges a reflection of the bridge's painted metal swam in the water.

" We could leave," Bobby said, his grip tightening on mine.

" Leave?"

His voice quickened in excitement. " Give it all up, yes. I've been thinking about it. We could sail out of reach of everyone else and start again."

" You mean give up our jobs?"

" Yes. Haven't you ever wanted to do that? To just, you know, pack it all in?"

" Leave our families?"

"Yes."

" But our children -"

" They would forget us. We could forget them. They'll survive. In fact, they'll be better off without us. We've done nothing but squabble with the people we're married to. Our kids would be better without that constant bickering and aggression. We would bring nothing of them with us, not even photographs. That would be the best way. We would live for ourselves and not for others. Why not? We could do what we've always wanted to do -- use our talents rather than fritter them away. There would be a living in it, we both know there would. We would be happier, more contented, maybe even richer."

" You would take a chance like that?"

" Yes. And you?"

I said nothing.

" We should be *with* each other," Bobby

insisted, freighting the word with emphasis.

We came to the end of the barges and stopped beside the last. Inside one of its dusty windows there was a handwritten For Sale sign. On the green bows there was a name painted in coal-black with a vivid red outline - *With*. It echoed Bobby's most intensely emphasised word.

He turned to me with a look that was both focused and distant, as if he were lost within a ferocious dream.

" Don't you see?" he asked. " This is no accident. We were meant to come here."

I shook my head. " It's just coincidence, Bobby. There must always be a barge or two for sale. As for the name -"

" We shouldn't turn away from this. We'll regret it for the rest of our lives if we do."

" Yes," I said after a short pause, " maybe you're right."

The yard manager was a small, burly man who was indifferent to the smudge of grease on his forehead. We sat in a cramped office, untidy with documentation and unidentifiable parts of engines, while he lit a cigarette and told us about the *With*. The previous owner had been a Dutchman called van something-or-other. His last name was too difficult to pronounce so everyone just called him Van. He'd drowned last year. They'd lifted him out of the canal with a boathook. Dead two days. It had been no surprise. Van's bargemanship had always been amateurish.

" He had no idea, really," he summed up, glancing at the ownership certificate before he passed it across the littered desk. A powdery cylinder of cigarette ash lay on the top page. I brushed it away to read the name.

" Johannes van Jaarsveld."

" If you say so, darling. He owed money on the barge. In fact Van had debts all along the canal."

" What about his relatives?" I asked.

" Couldn't be traced."

" You mean there was no address book or anything like that?"

The manager shifted in his chair. " None found," he said. " He could have destroyed it beforehand, of course."

" Why would he do that?"

" Search me."

" It was suicide, wasn't it?"

" Don't think so. Accidental death, that's what the coroner said."

I smiled.

" We said we'd sell the barge as soon as the legal boys were satisfied. There was a bit of trouble sorting out its name. It wasn't called the *With* originally. Van was the one who named it that - God knows why. Personal associations I suppose. You never knew with Van. He always kept himself to himself."

" The name lasted longer than he did," Bobby said. " It seems only fair to keep it. Anyways, I like it. It's unusual. And appropriate."

" Up to you."

" We haven't agreed this," I warned Bobby. " We were just finding things out."

Bobby smiled as if my caution were only token.

The manager became confidential. " You'd be getting a good buy. Besides, there are Van's clothes and books and all his bits and pieces thrown in."

" Didn't anyone else want them?" I asked.

" Not that lot, darling," he answered with a suddenly honest grin. " His clothes aren't fit to give away. As for his books, who's interested in the history of Holland?"

We returned within three weeks, bruised but exhilarated, and sailed as soon as we could. We had torn ourselves free. Like empty houses or discarded clothes, lives that we had thought would last forever now lay behind us. In the comforting gloom of that first night aboard the barge, we were truly beyond the reach of our pasts. All around, protecting us like a fortress, like a huge shell, the *With* lay dark and massive in the water.

In the small hours we were woken by the sound of rain. Bobby insisted we go out onto the top of the barge. I felt my nipples tighten, and hugged my arms to my breasts. The air was filled with the smell of canal water and weeds. All the blossoms on the trees were closed. Like the opening of a shutter, sliding rainclouds disclosed a brilliant moon.

We looked at each other. We were as pale as the drowned, and around us the fields and trees were the colour of ash and ivory. As we watched, a white stallion walked silently to the towpath fence and stood looking at us with fathomless black eyes. To raise our voices would have been to break a spell, so Bobby whispered.

" This is a new start for you. Remember the detail. Tomorrow you must paint it."

On the next day we came to a ladder of locks ascending the flank of a grassy escarpment. From below they resembled the bulwarks of wooden ships, stacked one inside the other. It took several hours to reach the highest. While we moved upwards, lock by lock, I tried to solve the technical problems of representing a horse in moonlight. But I could not, and instead I began to daydream. Meanwhile Bobby quickly sketched pen portraits of other barge owners and tried to sell them. There was some interest but no takers.

When we reached the uppermost lock we looked out across the valley as if from the deck of a galleon. The canal led straight towards the ladder, its water shining so that it resembled a long sword laid flat among the trees and fields. At that moment I was certain that we really had left our pasts behind forever.

On the next day we began to search through Van's belongings. There was little to salvage. His clothes were so rancid that we dumped them at the next refuse collection point. The crockery was chipped and the cutlery dulled, but we agreed to use them until we could buy replacements. Each book was at least thirty years old, and most dated from two or three decades before that. If lifted to the nostrils, they smelled of mould. There were also drawers full of fuse wire, playing cards, plugs, nails, screws, and pens with dried ink, most of which we threw away. At the back of one drawer Bobby found a black-and-white photograph, faded and unframed. Proud but uneasy in the presence of a camera, a woman and two young children stared out at us. They were high-cheekboned, old-fashioned, stolid.

I thought of the photographs taken of my own children, of how they had smiled, of how I had posed with them for my husband as he arranged every shot with a finicky precision.

" Your friend Van had someone after all," Bobby said.

" His family?"

" Wife and kids, don't you think?"

" Or perhaps that boy is Van, that's his sister, and that's their mother. It could be. It fits. Look at the style of their clothing."

" Maybe. I think it's his wife or his girlfriend."

" Bobby, we don't know and never will do, not now. Whoever they are there's not much point in keeping it."

" Look at their expressions. I could never draw expressions like that. They're too complex. And we shouldn't throw it out. Don't you agree?"

" We brought no mementoes of our own families. Why should we keep van Jaarsveld's?"

A thought struck him. " Is *With* a Dutch surname? Her name could be *With*."

" You're suggesting the barge was named after this woman?"

" Could be."

" You've no reason to think that."

" You never know. If it was, it would be wrong to throw her photo out. We should frame it instead. Put it on display."

" I don't think it would be wrong."

"More than wrong. It would be a kind of - well, a kind of sacrilege."

And Bobby returned the photograph to the drawer as if he were expecting someone to claim it.

I turned to the books. Most of them had been published in Holland, and seemed to be all histories and biographies.

" I don't know anything about any of this," I admitted.

" You're not the only one. That's why his books weren't sold after he died. No one's interested. Maybe we should learn Dutch sometime, when we've nothing better to do."

" And when will that be?"

Bobby hesitated a moment and then smiled.

"Never," he said.

At the far right of a shelf, wedged between the books and the bulkhead, there was a cardboard box file with battered corners. I took it down but hesitated.

" Open it," Bobby said, " it's not a booby

trap."

Inside was a ragged sheaf of papers held in place by a rusting spring clip. The topmost paper was handwritten in English. I read it aloud.

"*The Nature Of Conflict*. But it started off being called *The Nature Of War*."

Bobby peered over my shoulder, resting his chin on my collarbone and holding my waist in his hands.

"You can't say he wasn't ambitious," he murmured.

Releasing the clip, I lifted van Jaarsveld's papers from the box and spread them across the table. Soon I found a summary of points - *Sieges and Blockades: The Aftermath of Defeat; Failed Leaders: A Justification*, and so on. Each heading had been scratched out and amended several times as if Van had never been able to finally decide on the titles.

The pages of text were even more confused. Often he had begun to write in Dutch and then changed to English. Whole sections seemed to be translations or verbatim copies from the books on the shelves. These were interspersed with Van's own thoughts. Whenever he wrote in English they were derivative, badly-written sentences about the character of aggression, conflict, and warfare.

"Listen to this," I said.

"Astonish me," Bobby said drily.

"Here goes. *When individuals, peoples and nations come into conflict, their lives can never return to what they once were.*"

Bobby giggled.

"What's wrong?" I asked, although I knew why he had laughed.

"It's not what you would call blindingly original, is it? It sounds like a fifth-form essay. Assembling this rubbish must have taken him years. Just think of all that wasted time and energy. Our Dutch friend would have been much better off doing something else."

Suddenly Bobby and I must have each thought the same thing. We looked at each other and said nothing. We had no need of words. I had done no painting. Now that I was free of my husband and children I had begun to lose my ambition. I did not even need to ask Bobby about his own work. Apart from his sketches at the locks, I had seen no evidence of any having been done.

Quietened, shamed, we began to hurry through Van's notes. We took refuge in his repetitions, banalities, plagiarisms. I had an unpleasant taste in my mouth, but it did not stop me sneering at things a lonely man had worked on for years.

And then I became angry. At first I thought that my anger sprang from guilt because of the way we were misusing the notes, but very quickly I realised that it was because of Bobby's comments on the photograph. Weeks ago, he had persuaded me that the name *With* was both a good omen, a symbol. Now he seemed to believe that it memorialised a woman in Van's undiscoverable past. The anger camouflaged my growing conviction that both Bobby and I had been naive. The barge name was just a name, that was all. It had no significance beyond that.

" It's a stupid name, *With*," I said.

" Oh, come on."

" It's true. I never really liked it. Why couldn't van Jaarsveld have called the barge after his home town? Or his girlfriend's first name, or his mother's? People were right to be wary of him. He must have been obviously eccentric. He may as well have called his boat *Until* or *Next* or *From*. They would have made as much sense."

Bobby's answer was unexpectedly reflective.

" I don't think he was mad. I think that something just got the better of him, that's all. That's why he gave up. He just couldn't see any alternative to ending it all."

Although I was infuriated by Van, Bobby was growing more sympathetic. Whatever the Dutchman's failings, and however lonely, my lover was fascinated by him, and was beginning to find his obsessions seductive.

For the next few days a listless heat and humidity built around us. Thousands of tiny insects swarmed above the canal as it grew a film of algae and oil which absorbed light. We lolled silently in the enervating heat. Often Bobby sat motionless in the bows and stared down into the water as if trying to read messages within it. I wondered what imaginings occupied his mind. Whenever he was lost in thought, Bobby was unapproachable.

I kept the notes. Bobby had insisted we keep the photograph of the woman and children; that alone prevented me from throwing out Van's sheaves of paper. Instead I spent time looking through them, searching for a thread of logic, a gleam of achievement among the dislocated phrases and thickets of quotation. I found nothing. Van had left behind a jumble which he had never been able to shape. To pick up a page at random, and to begin to read it, was to enter ways with neither pattern nor centre.

Sometimes I thought there must be one page, perhaps even only one paragraph, which would explain everything, and that once I found it I would have a key to everything. But no such page and no such paragraph could be found.

And sometimes I felt that I was failing a test, and was convinced that there must be some kind of structure, a subtle argument that I was unable to see, let alone follow. Van had been well-read, an accumulator and sifter of fact and opinion, a man who might have taken his own life because of the enormity of his despair. Perhaps my own mind was too sluggish for a quicksilver intellect, my understanding too blunt for the fine detail of a masterwork.

It was to be expected, I thought glumly. I had led too unadventurous a life. I had become conditioned to restriction. I had not even been able to sustain the pleasure I had felt at our escape.

Bobby sat in the bows, hunched as if he were reading a book, and did not respond when I called his name. I spread Van's notes on the table again. here it all was - quotations, names, dates, scraps of history, biography, meditation. No mention of anyone or anything called *With*.

I persevered for about fifteen minutes and then gave up and walked towards Bobby along the side of the barge. The sun was a flat white disc sunk beneath the water. Bobby did not move, although he must have heard me coming up behind him.

" Bobby," I said softly, and he turned towards me.

His face was pale and strained, and in his hand was a photograph. For a second I thought it was of the woman, but then I saw it was in colour. My heart lurched. It was of Bobby and his own two children. His boy, his girl.
Their clear, open faces looked outwards, smiling as if there was no doubt over their future.

" We agreed not to bring any photographs," I said.

" Yes, he agreed, in a voice so small it was scarcely audible.

"It was your idea, Bobby. No mementoes, no souvenirs, not even memories. That's what you said."

"Van Jaarsveld deserted his family as well. But he named the barge after his wife, so he would never forget, so he would always be reminded of her."

"We don't know that."

Bobby said nothing.

"That photograph might have had nothing to do with Van or his wife," I insisted. "We have no idea who he named the barge after, or if it was named after anyone. For God's sake, there's no need to be romantic about this."

Bobby went on as if I had not spoken.

"He gave up things of value in return for a heap of paper. We were drawn to the *With*. It wasn't just an accident. When we were told about Van, we must both have recognised we were just like him - hopeless, foolish daydreamers."

I did not answer, but made my way back along the side of the barge. Bobby turned away from me and looked ahead.

Van Jaarsveld's papers lay strewn around the table. I picked among them morosely, and then was suddenly enraged at their number, their misplaced energy. I hated Van's self-pity, his suicide, his domestication of his own failure. I hated the name he had given the barge, I hated the insoluble mystery which had given Bobby so much latitude for his own fantasies.

I picked up a handful of papers. "Bobby!" I shouted down the barge, "Bobby!"

If he had asked me I would have placed the papers back in the file, but he did not even move.

I let them tumble over the side. They spilled out across the canal, their words softening and becoming faint beneath the oily sheen on the water.

Once I had done this I wanted to be rid of them

all. I began to scoop up further handfuls and throw them overboard. They floated behind us, fanning out behind us like the signs of some vast and terrible battle. For a moment I believed I saw the name de With, but then another sheet settled on top of the writing, water slipped across the surfaces, and it vanished forever, leaving only its puzzle.

When there were no notes left I picked up the empty box file and threw that into the water too. It floated for a minute, then filled and sank. I sat down, feeling weak and feverish.

Bobby sat motionless in the bows, staring ahead.

Slowly, purposefully, the *With* was approaching a bridge with green metal struts.

New Fiction from the North

And Nobody Knew She Was There
Fiona Cooper

She stood at the window all day watching.Then it was night-time and all the lights went down.
" Are ya all reet, pet? Daen't worry, daen't worry, bairn, we'll all look after ye!"
     Skinny white fingers prodded her cheeks and the sick green glow of the all night light made a hallowe'en mask of the ancient face hanging over her like death. The words came out rusty, distorted by toothless gums and dementia.
" When ye hear the siren, Ah'll tek ye doon th'Anderson and ye'll be safe, bonny bairn, we'll be safe together, so we will!"
She froze. Best pretend to be asleep or the hands would go on and on, patting and prodding, twisting her hair, making her sheets into swaddling bands, binding her to the bed as sure as the leather straps riveted to the bed frame.
No place for a bairn.
     Eleven ancient women institutionalised god knows how long or why. She was the bairn and it wasn't right having her here, the nurses said, but what can you do.Nowhere to send bairns like her.
     The place was called Cherry Blossom House, and that was a pack of lies, any fool could tell. How can it be a house where none of the doors are locked apart from a double set leading outside? Doors in houses were locked, bedroom doors and the door under the stairs and the back door, locking her in, locking her out, locking

her away. And cherry blossom was her Dad in the kitchen with all the boots on a sheet of newspaper, humming and rubbing, cherry blossom was shoe polish, everyone knows that. The only polish here was scummy grey and the grey floors stank of piss and disinfectant. And she couldn't see her Dad, the police said it wasn't allowed. Not her Dad or her mam. For her own good, for your own good, pet, the judge has decided. She didn't mind about her mam, that was God being good to her, but it made her wild when they talked about her Dad.

They said it was him who'd put her there in Cherry Blossom House, talking as if she couldn't hear. Just because she didn't speak. She stood and listened and thought, you filthy old hag, you dirty mouthed old bastard. All the time she stared out of the window. There was a field outside with a white horse in it, running free. Her Dad took her riding and pinning her rosettes and certificates on the wall and her mam tossed the rosettes into the fire and tore the paper in two when he went out.

She counted the horse putting his left front hoof, one two three ... a hundred ... then she counted him putting down his right front hoof. One two three four five ...

Thirty-seven, thirty-eight, ye knaa, they say he burnt that bairn, burnt her wi a hot iron till the bone showed *forty-nine, fifty,* they should burn him, ye knaa, a bit bairn like that, ee, it's a wicked world, there'll be plenty of flames where his sort is gannin'

Three hundred and one he never did, that was me mam, you stupid old cow, three hundred and five, me dad loves me and they'll not let him see us.

Going to the toilet was worst. Even her mam would never burst in on her going to the toilet. Well, she would, she'd do anything, her mam, but so far she

51

hadn't and she wasn't allowed anywhere near her. Here there were three toilets with no seats, all in a room with no partitions between them and a doorway to the room with no door in it. And the old ladies would go in, their dresses all hitched up already as they spun down the corridor like pinballs in slow motion, banging walls and rapping their heads with their knuckles. They sat on the high porcelain rims singing and swearing at the top of their voices.
" Ah'd tek me knickers doon for that doctor, me!"
" Ee, d'ye mind the touch of a man getting hot wi ye?"
" Friggin' filthy ould cow!"
" Ah've heard ye'd drop yer drawers fer owt in trousers, ye!"
" There's been more driven through ye than the friggin' Tyne Tunnel!"
" Shut yer bloody filthy gob, the bairn's standin' listenin' to yez!"
" Aah, the bairn. She's a bonny bairn."
" Aah, pet, ye're ower young to knaa aboot it, ye'll knaa aboot it soon enough. Just remember this, be a good bairn and divent ever let a man get his hands in yer knickers, for that's when the trouble begins."
" Aah, that's awful, talking like that tae a bairn!"
" It's the truth!"
" It is an' all!"

And the skinny arms reached out to her, skirts all rucked up, bloomers hanging round bony ankles, stockings sagging round ankles swollen with fluid, and arses tethered to the white porcelain and she stood in the stink of it and said nothing. One old lady walked every morning to the toilet and sat without taking her knickers down. When she stood up she smiled and walked to the door stinking of shit and piss and shouted:
" NURSE! NURSE!"
Dear, dear, what can the matter be?

The bairn, the poor bairn, she used the staff toilet, it wasn't allowed but when they stopped her she just sat and pissed where she was sitting until they said, It's not right, a bairn wi all these basket cases, we'll turn a blind eye.

Years later she knew it was love, all the touching and hugging, the patting and poking and crooning and mad lullabies screeched at three in the morning: it was love. She was a bairn and they were old women who'd had bairns and never seen them, or had bairns they never saw, or never had bairns at all. But she was twelve when they put her in Cherry Blossom House and it scared her witless.

Although they never shouted at her, never hit her, never hurt her, it was all nursery rhymes and stories and reaching out to touch her.

The worst was when she was just about asleep. Always when her eyes were just about closed.

" Gan tae sleep, bonny bairn, we'll all rock ye safe."

The one with the teeth, the one with five mad wisps of hair, the one they put in a jacket that pinned her arms down when she tore at her head. Standing over her, yellow nails trembling on her cheek. She balled her fists and clamped her teeth tight shut.

" Do you want an injection?"

The nurse in the doorway.

" Do you?"

" No, nurse, I don't want an injection, me."

" Do you want an injection, like?"

" No, no, no, not for me, nurse."

" DO YOU WANT AN INJECTION?"

Today he swished his tail four hundred and fifteen times go away she doesn't want an injection tomorrow he'll bend his head and crop the grass and this is Cherry Blossom House only there's no cherries and there's no blossom and it isn't a house. And she

doesn't want an injection, can't you hear her say no, stop asking her, stupid, stupid, what are you, deaf?
" Get to bed and let the poor bairn sleep, she's got enough troubles without you as a nightmare!"
" Gah!"

The nurse's shoes had rubber soles and they squeaked like pain driving the baldy old crow to her bed. Her gums bit her finger and she wailed and dribbled.
" I don't need strapping in, nurse, not tonight."
" One step out of bed and it'll be straps and an injection, I've warned you."
" I might need the toilet, nurse."
" Then you ask me. Mind you do."
" Toilet. Ask you. I don't want strapping in, nurse."

When the squeak of the shoes stopped and the nurse's door closed, they sang to her.
" Go to sleep my baby, close your pretty eyes ..."
" Shut yer friggin' trap, man, I want to sleep!"
" The lights is all oot! Is it a blackout?"
" Blackout! I'll punch yer friggin' lights oot for ye!"
" Poor bairn!"
" It's a shame!"
" He wants locking up and the key hoyed doon the netty!"
" I'll hoy ye doon the netty if ye divven shut yer mouth the neet!"

Even when they stopped wailing and caterwauling and talking and singing and wandering, there was noise. Old gums sucking thumbs, screams from bad dreams, weeping in their sleep. One woman didn't close her eyes all night, a thin woman who never spoke, just like her. She lay all night staring into the green glow.

Some days, not every day, not regularly, a newspaper came onto the ward. An old lady who said

she'd been a schoolteacher used to read it out loud from front to back, including the adverts.
" Send today, three and six, for your spring selection of bulbs, allow twenty eight days for delivery."
" How does your garden grow?" sang a wispy shadow of a woman who watered her plants all round the ward every day from the unbreakable plastic beakers.
" Aren't the tulips coming on lovely, do you like the red ones, do you think they're pretty, bonny bairn?"

Her shaking hand pointed to the dribbles of water on the floor where it met the wall.

Every day the cleaners shouted at her:
" Will ye stop hoying water on the floor, ye daft ould bat, we divent knaa if it's piss or water and we hev to clean the bugger up and there's not the time!"
" It's water," she told them patiently, " It's good clean water, what else but water would I put on my bonny flowers?"

She beckoned the bairn, *they're crackerjacks*, she told her, *crackerjacks, they say they cannot see my bonny garden, do you like red tulips, bonny bairn, I'll pick them for ye*.
" Now is the time for spring-cleaning," the school teacher read, " And where better to start than last year's wardrobe? Brighten up last year's summer frock with an applique motif. Cross stitch a border or daisies on a plain skirt to say that summer's on the way."

The old ladies pleated their blue serge hems and one of them started dancing, here we go round the mulberry bush, she sang.
" Printed in England," said the schoolteacher, " Now then."

They weren't allowed scissors or knives in Cherry Blossom House, but the schoolteacher folded knife-edge creases into the sheets of newspaper and cut along with a hair-grip or the handle of a pilfered

spoon. All they wanted was pictures of babies, pictures of little children and they stuck them up everywhere.
" That's me," said old baldy, pointing to a chubby infant with a balloon.
" Was I not a bonny baby, eh, wasn't I then?"
" Ye hed mair hair on yer head then than now, ye mad bat!"
" Take no notice, bairn," said old baldy, " She says that's her when she was young, that one there, with all the dark curls. Ye knaa! She's a bit screwy, bairn, pay no mind, lookit, her hair's straight as a plank and white as snow!"
" At least I've a head of hair!"
" Empty barns divent need thatching, come here, bonny bairn, I've summat to tell ye."

She spoke so nice, this one, with a scottish lilt, she told the bairn about her granny's home in the highland hills.
" One night," she promised, " One night they'll forget to lock the doors and I'll come and tap on your bed and we'll go. I'll not speak because they'll hear me. We'll go to my granny's house in Scotland. They tell me it's burnt to the ground, they say I burnt it down! But I know different. I know where it is. Why would I burn my granny's house down? That's where we'll go, bonny bairn, for there's lots of wicked men in this world, a lot of wicked men."

The schoolteacher took her hand and walked her round the ward.
" They're all mad as birds, my bonny lass," she told her, " Her and her granny's house in Scotland! She's been here since she was sixteen years old! I know."
Why are you here, the bairn wondered, for the school teacher made sense all the time, until the doctor came, when she started to mutter and scream and scrub her palms against her face.

" She's been fine," the nurses said, " Fine until this morning, doctor, maybe we should give her a shot?"
" Put her down on the list," the doctor said good-naturedly.

The list was everyone lining up at the open doorless doorway over the passage every week for electric shock treatment, they seemed to want it, to like it, but maybe it was just something a bit different. A bit of a change.

After she wet herself for three days, after she threw her plate on the floor, they threatened her with the electric, but the doctor said no, no, we're still not sure what good it does, not sure what it does at all, no. Maybe as a last resort.

Everyone had electric except her and the thin woman who never spoke or looked up from the floor. There were days when the others started, it'll be a day of divilment, the nurses said, it's the weather. They locked her and the thin woman in the office, locked the ward doors and called in the men.
" Here we go again, it's the floorshow!"

A chair would splinter against the wall and a tiny old woman with red eyes laughed and picked up the end of a metal bed. *There she goes!* Or old baldy would knot a sheet and swing it like a whip and a cudgel all in one and god help everyone.

And the men came in and there was screaming and later the nurses let them out, her and the thin woman. In the ward, some were strapped into bed, some were mummified in tight wet sheets and some sat drugged and drooling.
" Mebbes we can have a bit peace now!" said the nurses.

One had glasses and the others would take it in turns to swipe them from her nose and jeer and taunt.
" I'll stamp these underfoot and then we'll see ye in

trouble, ye blind old bat!"

And the old lady with bad eyes and worse legs would totter from the chair wailing no, no, give them here, ye witch, give them back, they're mine.

One old lady cried all the time and when the nurses said, all gentle and kind, like you talk to a child, like her mam talked to her sister and brother -
" Come on now, pet, let's get you dressed,"
- she would weep so that tears splashed off her skinny shoulders and say very quietly *no, please don't, no, please don't do that, please, I don't want you to do that to me, oh please, I'd rather you didn't*

That was worse than all the piss pot throwing and hurling of tin plates and fragile fists bleeding from hitting the metal radiator and the walls. *Please don't, please, please don't.* And it was everything, getting dressed, going to the toilet, having baths, eating, sitting, walking, sleeping. *Please, oh please don't.*

There were baths. Ordinary baths only no doors, and towels stiff as leather stamped HOSPITAL PROPERTY. The women screamed and flailed their arms for bathtime. Especially for the three baths with rubber sheets over the tops and pipes like white scaleless snakes all around them. Three nurses strong-armed old baldy into the snake bath and fixed the top down and switched it on.
" AAH! It's got me, it's getting me, help, NURSE!"

Only her head showed, her wispy head with its caved in mouth, screaming. She thought, the bairn, she thought that snakes came out of the pipes and writhed along on bare flesh, beetles came out and crawled and scorpions rattled along bare legs and stung. So when they put her in she didn't scream - screaming was the same as talking - she fought like fury and threw her head from side to side to bite at the hands stripping her, tying her under the rubber sheet.

" Pet, there's a lot worse than having a hydro, wad ye credit it, the bairn's terrified."
" It's them ould loonies screeching has put the fear of God in her."
" And no wonder. Poor bairn."

She shrank into her body against the snakes and though it felt like water, there were water snakes too, she knew that, water snakes wriggling blind from the white pipes. It was water, water writhing like snakes until she passed out cold before the beetles came.
An old lady stalked into the toilet room and sat on the white porcelain bowl with her knickers on. After a few minutes she stood up and stalked to the door. Piss splashed her stockings, she stank of shit, she rubbed the bairn's head and said merrily, like you might say isn't it a lovely day, she said:
" Oh, dear, pooped again! NURSE!"

They had breakfast. They poured cornflakes and milk into a bowl with the glasses at the bottom.

Ah cannot see the day, ah cannot see what Ah'm eating, ye're all trying to poison me, I need me glasses. NURSE!

They made a sandwich with a stray pair of false teeth.

Yez friggin' bastard ould cunts. Ah cannot eat me breakfast wi'oot me teeth, I'll choke! NURSE!

They chewed and took it out of their mouths and showed it and laughed and dropped it on the floor and slid off the chair and ate from the grey piss and disinfectant tiles. They drank each other's tea in gulps and pinched each other's bread and cursed and used salt for sugar.
" Do you want an injection?"

They flicked spoonfuls of soggy cornflakes at old baldy. She smiled like a madonna and massaged it into her wispy scalp, blowing toothless kisses round the room.

Later that day she stood at the window - ee the poor bairn, it's wicked - *five hundred and seventy* and the doctor came up to her.

" Do you like horses?"

Five hundred and seventy five, five hundred and seventy six and a mouthful of daisies.

" They're lovely creatures, aren't they?"

Five hundred and eighty one, five hundred and eighty two.

" She's a beauty, that mare."

" She's not a mare," she said, what a fool he was, "That's a stallion."

One two three four five
Once I caught a fish alive ...

She froze.

" Oh, you are in there, are you?" the doctor said quietly.

Alive, alive - oh!

Shut your trap!

He'd got her, caught her like some daft little tiddler on a hook, yanked from the deep forest green of weeds and water: a flick of the wrist and it's high above the stream bed, out of the cool wetness and into dry hot air, hanging from a metal hook and gasping. Landed.

I've landed myself in it now, this is the worst, now they'll never leave me alone, now I've spoken, there'll be visitors, God help me, somebody help me, visitors. And then they'll send me home and she'll be there, and everywhere I go, her cruel eyes and the words and her hands hitting me, pulling my hair, dragging my arms, she'll use anything that comes to hand. Oh, doctor, I'm in trouble. I'll never speak again, I promise, I swear.

Outside in the sunshine, the white stallion swished at flies.

Six
seven
eight nine ten
then I let it go again
      She stood at the window, the bairn, the poor bairn, she stood at the window watching, glass and the bars between her and the world outside.

New Fiction from the North

Geographicals
Julia Darling

When I was drinking, I would get on planes and think that would solve everything, like when I went to Canada.
I just emptied a drawer of underwear into a suitcase. I thought that I wanted to be somewhere big. I was already drunk when I limped onto the plane. My clothes were creased and dirty. I was sitting right at the back, next to a man who filled up the whole seat, and who kept on poking about in his bag. I couldn't undo the stiff little pack of butter next to my bread roll. I asked him to help me. He was huge, with shoulders like a bull. He unwrapped the golden foil, even though his fingers were much bigger than mine.
He asked me where I was from and I told him, England, and he said London? And I was squashing the butter across the bread roll with the plastic knife, and saying, no, North. North, I said again, and the knife broke. He laughed and lent me his knife. Is that Leeds? he asked. No, Newcastle, I told him. Football. It's everywhere. Nightclubs. Black and white. Shearer!
I don't watch football he said. Cricket's my game.
I haven't got a game, I said.
He asked me what I did, as the air hostess bent over us both with a silver teapot and I asked her how she managed not to spill things, and I could see her thinking, we've got a right one here.
I'm a dancer, I told him.
A dancer, he said, in a kind, interested voice. What kind of dance?

Contemporary, I trilled, but I hurt my ankle. I didn't tell him about falling off the stage. No, I didn't tell him that, and anyway, I don't remember it very well, just the landing part, the soft feeling of people's hands trying to catch me, the hissing silence when the music stopped.

I wanted to tell him about when I was nineteen, and how sharp and agile I was, but I didn't. I drank my wine and my tea at the same time, and I asked him what he did.

I sell alarms, he said, all over the world.

What kind of alarms? I asked him.

All sorts. Mainly buildings.

So I told him about being burgled, and how I wished that I'd had an alarm, because it had made me really paranoid, like there was no point getting fond of anything because it would just get spoilt or lost, and he said quietly, I know what you mean.

Are you going to drink that wine? I asked him, because he hadn't touched the plastic bottle of Chardonnay on his tray, and he said, go on, have it. I don't drink.

It's just that I'm afraid of flying, I said. That's why I have to drink.

You go ahead, he said. It makes it worse though. You'll see.

Not me, I said. For me it makes things better.

Perhaps you'll sleep, he said in his soft voice. You look tired.

And I felt a burst of fondness for this man with his boulder face and American chest. I thought about his house. It would have big rooms. Maybe six or seven bedrooms, a big woody garden, and a cavernous deep freeze full of sides of beef. Perhaps he'd have a weekend log cabin somewhere up a mountain, and a gun and a hairy comfortable dog. I asked him if he'd got children and he told me he'd got a daughter called Sally

Ann, but she lived in New York, and he hadn't seen her for a while.
We talked about New York, and I told him about going to the bar where Dylan Thomas drank his last drink, and how the beer was awful. And he laughed.
Then we sat quietly for a while, in comfortable silence, with the aeroplane humming and droning, and outside there was a heavenly landscape of bubbly clouds, and our faces were caught in this warm pink light. The air hostess, who was blonde and plump, came and took away our food trays, and he said, by the way, they call me Greg, and held out his hand, and I put my thin sweaty hand into his and told him that my name was Stella. His hand was enormous.
I told him I didn't like my name.
Choose another one, he said.
You look a bit like my daughter, he told me. She's thin like you, and to tell you the truth Stella, I'm worried about her. The last time she called me on the phone she said she was fine, but I know she wasn't telling me the truth. I'm a salesman, and it's my business to know when people are telling the truth. I don't know what's the matter with her. Could be drugs. I haven't heard from her for a while. She's disappeared. And his face fell into heavy folds of sadness.
The wine was making everything seem soft and hot.
Why don't you go and look for her? I said.
I've tried, he said. I look for her everywhere. Seeing you, it makes me think of her, that's all.
The film was starting. It was all about guns and men kicking doors in, and the blonde air hostess was tucking us all up, pulling down the blinds and switching off the lights. The plane quietened as we plugged in our headphones and settled down under our blankets.
The aeroplane itself seemed to sleep. At one point, in the dark, I murmured, Where are we?

We're flying over the North Pole, he whispered; a long way from home.
I tried to shut my eyes but I couldn't sleep. I watched bits of the film but it didn't make much sense. The characters were barking instead of speaking. Greg was lying back in his seat with his mouth wide open. I had an urge to close his mouth. It looked like a door left open. Some time passed. I climbed past Greg and staggered to the toilet. I sat on the seat and read all the notices about smoking and hand cream, and drank from the bottle of vodka in my handbag. When the toilet flushed it sounded angry, like it wanted to suck me out of the plane and spit me into the atmosphere. When I got back to my seat. Greg was lolling forwards, and I tried to gently push him back. That's when I noticed that he was a funny colour, and that his eyes were half closed and that he was making an odd squeaking sound. I pushed the alarm button, and looked wildly up and down the aisle. The blonde air hostess came up to me, and I said to her, he's not well, but my voice was like sludge, and she looked at me as if I was dirt.
I don't know what's the matter with him, I said. She became efficient, bending over and listening to his chest, behaving as if she was doing something she'd been taught on a course. She called a steward. I staggered backwards, and landed next to a woman and a baby. The baby stared at me with tear stained cheeks. Do you know him? asked the air hostess.
His name is Greg, I said, we only just met. Is he dead? He's had a heart attack, she told me, we'll have to lie him down. The steward and the air hostess heaved Greg from his seat. He flopped about, and his face was rusty and worn out. She lay him on the floor and started to give him the kiss of life. The steward went to see the pilot. Everyone was waking up and looking worried. The baby started to whimper.

I sat there and wished I had a drink. Even at a time like that I thought of myself. The pilot spoke to us in a calm carpeted voice. He said that we would have to land, that a man was ill, and that he needed medical attention. The passengers sighed collectively. They were inconvenienced. Greg looked a bit better. He was breathing normally. I felt guilty. Like everything I touched got spoilt.

The plane began to descend and the blonde air hostess wiped her forehead, wishing she was on another shift. I looked out of the window. White light sliced into the plane. Below us there was nothing but snow; a huge featureless desert of snow. The plane flew lower and lower, like an albatross with heavy beating wings.

Wow! said someone behind me. Look at that!

I'd never seen anywhere so empty and white. It was like landing in the middle of nothing.

Something in me was afraid of that landscape.

The plane doors opened, and bright freezing air gusted in. Some men came in wearing fur jackets and sunglasses. Their hair was dark and long and pulled back into pony tails. I think they were Eskimos. They had a truck waiting down on the snowy runway, and they dragged Greg onto a stretcher and covered him up with a blanket. He was awake. I leant over and touched his arm. You'll be alright, I told him, looks like you've landed. And he smiled at me, and said, look after yourself Stella. Then he said, where the hell am I?

The North Pole, I told him.

I always wanted to go to the North Pole, he said.

He fumbled in his pocket and pulled out a card. Stella, he said, phone my wife. Would you do that? I took the card and nodded.

Then they carried him out and closed the doors, and the pilot made a joke about having a free trip to the ice wastes, and the plane soared back into the air. Next to me Greg's seat was very empty, as if the emptiness was as big as he was.

When we landed at Toronto I went straight to the telephone. I dialled the number on the card, while other people pushed past, trying to get places. I heard a voice answering at the other end, and it was a woman, and she was saying, Greg is that you? And then she was saying Sally Ann? Who's there? And I was pushing money into the slot, but some of the coins rolled onto the floor, and I scrambled about trying to find them, and the phone went dead.

So I went to the airport bar and smoked and drank. I fell off the stool. I found myself in tears, telling the bartender about Greg, about the North Pole, and he was young and Canadian and he said, don't you think you've had enough? And I repeated what he said. I said to myself that I'd had enough. I wandered out into the airport lounge and fell asleep on a plastic seat, like falling down a dark hole.

And then I dreamt I was back in that icy endless landscape where everything was white and there were no edges.

I was standing there wearing soft shoes, that were unsuitable for snow. I put one foot carefully in front of the other, and my foot disappeared. I could feel the coldness trickling in between my shoe and my sock, like a sharp pain. The aeroplane was waiting for me, with its' engines running, and its' interior looked bright and cheerful. I could see Greg looking out of the window and smiling, telling me to hurry up. I put my other foot in front of the first one, and the snow made a satisfying crunch, almost a squeak. Greg was calling my name "Stella!" silently through the thick glass. I pulled my thin coat around me, but I couldn't move quickly enough, and the plane door was taking off, and I was left there, both feet stuck, immobilised, like I'd fallen down a crack, like I'd never get home, with just the memory of where the plane had been, the disruption of the air, the squawking of lonely birds, feeling the outer edges of my heart beginning to harden and grow icy cold.

I woke up. An Indian cleaner was prodding my shoulder, making a slushing sound like rustling leaves. I remembered that I was in Canada. I went to the ladies and washed my face again and again, and then I combed my hair. I took the bottle of vodka from my handbag and poured it down the basin.

Then I went searching for another telephone. This time it was in a quiet corner of the airport, and I dialled the number again, very slowly and carefully. The woman answered and her voice was hard and cold. You don't know me, I said. I met your husband on a plane. He asked me to call.

He's dead, she said. He died an hour ago.

I'm so sorry, I said. He was a really nice man. There was a long, deep silence, as wild and white as the endless landscape of snow.

Who are you? she said eventually.

For a palpable moment I forgot my name.

Stella, I blurted at last. I was just the person sitting next to him, that's all.

I can't feel anything, she said. It's not real. I can't talk to you now.

And she hung up, and I looked at my shaking hand holding the receiver, and then I stared at the people around me in the airport, with their bags of possessions, trying to get from one place to another.

I went back to the flight desk, and I asked for a ticket home, back to Newcastle, back to the North. The woman looked at me with half her face, as if she wasn't sure if I was serious.

Didn't you like it here? she asked me. You haven't been

anywhere yet.
I've been to the North Pole, I told her. I've seen enough. I want to go home.

New Fiction from the North

The Full Monty
──────── *Chrissie Glazebrook*

I've got Mrs Shiner for my community project. Mrs Lucy Shiner. She lives just round from Jade, in the old folks' bungalows behind the Ritz Bingo.

'You'll enjoy talking to her,' Miss Petty says. 'She's quite lucid, for her age.'

Lucy Lucid. Lucky me.

'I'm trusting you to be respectful,' says Miss Petty. She's trimmed the hairs on her mole. 'You're an ambassador of the school so remember to take your ID card and wear your blazer the first time you see her.'

Jade nearly wets herself when I tell her.

'Mad Lucy?' she says. 'She's a right nutter. Scare in the community. Mum reckons she's one step away from a bag lady.'

'No shit?' I goes.

What it is, right, we have to interview a Senior Citizen person and get them to talk about the olden days. Oral history, they call it. We have to do it in our summer holidays as well. Bummer or what?

It takes her for ever to answer the door. She doesn't even glance at my ID, I could be a homicidal maniac for all she knows. She looks mad-*ish*, but not totally mentalistic. She's hanging on to this walking-stick and there's lots of pink scalp showing through her hair.

'You must be ...'

Rose West. Myra Hindley.

'Becky,' I say. 'Becky Moon. From St Edwin's.'

'You're not the bath nurse?'
'No.'
The house smells of wee and that scent old wifies wear. It's a right clutterpit, too many chairs and loads of cushions and hundreds of glass animals. I feel a bit clausters. I sit in a hard chair with a slippy seat. Mrs Shiner doesn't say anything for ages, just stares out the window.

'Who did you say you are?'
Hannibal Lecter. Freddie Kreuger.
'I'm Becky. From St Edwin's. I'm doing a reminiscence project for school. The teacher came and explained about it at the Evergreen Club.'
'Oh yes, I remember. That young woman with the sharp face and the big mole.' She's not all that daft then.
'Miss Petty, yes.'
She shuffles about in the chair. I can hear her bones creaking.
'Where would you like me to start?' she says.
'Dunno. What about the war?' Bor-ing, but that's what we're supposed to say if they can't think of anything.

Mrs Shiner stares up at the ceiling for a bit, then starts pat-a-caking her hands like a baby. 'I know,' she says. 'I'll tell you about Monty.'
'Was he somebody famous in the war?' The name rings a bell.
'Oh, no. He was my little boy, my beautiful little boy.' Her eyes start to fill up. Miss Petty warned us about this, old folks blubbing when they start to remember stuff. I stare down at my feet. My Docs are real shiny, Mum made me clean them before I came out.

Mrs Shiner shuts her eyes and twiddles with her wedding ring. Talk about watching paint dry. I'm wondering whether to leg it, then her stomach starts gurgling like bathwater going down a plughole. She hodges herself up in the chair.

'I can't talk now, Becky, I'm worn out. I would like to tell you about Monty, though. You put me in mind of him somehow. It must be that lovely red hair.'

'California Sunset,' I say. 'Lasts through twelve shampoos.'

She smiles. 'I've never told a soul about Monty, not in all these years. Could you come Thursday? The warden will have collected my pension then.'

I meet Jade outside the Liquor Mart. We hang out there sometimes, hoping we can persuade someone to go in and buy some Hooch for us.

'What's yours like, then?' I ask. She got Mr Bainbridge from Byron Close.

Jade sniffs. 'Dirty lech, he plays pocket billiards all the time. I grassed the pervy old sod up to Miss Petty. She's put him on the blacklist so I've got to go down the Evergreen Club and pick another one. How's Mad Lucy?'

'Canny weird,' I say. I hope this Monty story's gonna be worth the grief.

She's got the tea on and some No Frills digestives from Kwik Save. Her hair's all fluffed up at the back and she's put powder on her face. She dives straight into the story.

'I'd just come out of hospital,' she says. 'I'd had a couple of misses, my insides were all to pot so they'd taken everything away.' Oldwifespeak for a hysterectomy, I know that much. 'You weren't allowed to pick up a kettle for weeks in those days. I just lay in bed getting depressed because I knew I could never have a bairn.'

I dunk a biscuit in my tea. It breaks off and sinks to the bottom of the cup.

'Edgar, that was my husband,' Mrs Shiner goes on, 'he said we should adopt a war baby. Those GIs dropped no end of girls in trouble, but I couldn't even think about it. That's when he said we should get a pet, a hamster or a budgie, something to keep me company while he was at the pit.'

I finish drinking my tea. The biscuit's all soggy in the bottom so I scoop it up on my finger and suck it.

'He wouldn't say where he got Monty from.' She's on a roll now. 'Some black market shenanigans, I reckon. He brought him home wrapped in a blanket. I thought it was a baby, till I saw all the hair. It took some getting used to, but after a while I thought real babies were the peculiar ones, just baldy pink skin.'

Shit, I forgot to bring a pen and paper. I swipe another digestive.

'What was he, then? Monty?'

She takes a slurp of cold tea. Some of it runs down her chin.

'We didn't know ourselves at first. We had to look him up in the encyclopaedia." There was a picture of a fully grown one, massive he was. Great long arms, big pot belly, all that magnificent red hair. Just like yours, Becky.'

I tug my fringe to see how long it is. I'm trying to grow it out, and it's taking for ever.

'What was he? A puppy?'

Mrs Shiner stares at me like I'm an eejit.

'An orang utan,' she says. 'From Borneo. They're different from the Sumatran ones. Know what it means, Becky? Orang utan? Old man of the woods.'

'Right.' Must try to remember that, to write down later.

'I dressed him in nappies, lovely fluffy terry-towelling nappies, not these paper things they have nowadays. I used to bath him in the sink and put baby powder on his bottom. He even went to sleep with a dummy in his mouth. He was my little baby. My son.'

She starts to drift off. I sit there for a minute or two, then take the tea things into her poky little kitchen, wash them up and put them away all neat. On the way out I pop my head round the door. She's making a purring noise like our cat.

'I'll come again Monday, Mrs Shiner. Same time, if that's OK.'

'Monday,' she mutters. 'All right, Becky.' Her head flops over to the side and she's asleep.

Jade comes round to ours to listen to my new Charlatans CD.

'I went down the Evergreen Club today,' she says. 'Couldn't get any of them to talk to me. They just wanted to play bingo, pathetic old sods. What about Mad Lucy?'

I sit at the dressing-table mirror and Oxycute my spots. 'You'll never guess,' I say. 'She used to have an orang utan. She brought it up like a baby.'

'A *monkey?*' gawps Jade.

'An ape,' I correct her. 'They're apes, orang utans.'

Jade snorts. 'Yeah, right. Told you she was off her trolley.' She watches me dab spot-killer on my chin. 'You don't believe that shit, do you? I'm telling you, Beck, old Lucy left the stadium yonks ago.'

But I do. I believe Mrs Shiner.

Three times I have to ring the doorbell. I hear a cloppy noise coming down the hall. Mrs Shiner's Zimmer frame.

'My legs are playing up,' she explains. Her face

is all scrunched up like a fist. I sit her down and stick the pouffe under her feet.

'Would you like a drink?' I offer.

She nods.

But the milk's gone off. I have a good skeg round the kitchen and eventually find some flat Lucozade, which is about all there is.

I remembered to bring my notepad this time.

'Monty was very bright,' says Mrs Shiner, cradling her drink. 'I tried to teach him to talk but of course he couldn't, they don't have the same vocal cords as us, but I swear he understood every word I said. He'd be on the floor playing with his bricks and I'd say, " Monty, come." He'd crawl over the floor, hold out his arms to be picked up and twine himself around me. Eee, Becky, it was the happiest time of my life.'

I write down, *'Monty Come. Cuddle. Mrs S happy'*.

'And his face, his lovely little face, you could tell what he was thinking by his eyes,' Mrs Shiner says. 'He had so much love in those eyes, and I adored him. I thought more of him than I did of Edgar, if truth be known. You know, Becky, when he was upset he used to crawl up inside my dress for comfort.'

'What, *Edgar?*'

'Monty.' She pulls a hanky out of her cardigan sleeve and blows her nose. She's blubbing but I pretend not to notice. I say I have to go but I'll see her on Wednesday. That brightens her up a bit.

'You're a good girl, Becky,' she says, stroking my hand.

'Can you put that in writing for my mum?' I say, and she laughs.

Jade's got the Blu-tack to stick up this huge poster of H out of Steps. She's done her hair in bunches like Britney Spears. She looks a right clip. 'You look wicked,' I tell her.

'I hate those bloody old gadges down the Evergreens,' she says. 'All they think about is bingo and scran. You ought to see them tucking into their dinners, it's gross, like feeding time at the zoo.'

We paint Stop 'n' Gro on our fingernails. Jade's got ten Regals so we spark up and blow the smoke out the window.

'Speaking of zoos,' says Jade, 'how's Crazywoman and the chimp?'

'Orang utan,' I correct her.

'Whatever,' shrugs Jade. 'Mum reckons when Mr Shiner snuffed it, old Lucy danced on his grave, singing her head off.'

'That's a crock of shit,' I say.

I borrow a fiver from Mum's purse and buy a carton of milk and some chocolate almonds for Mrs Shiner. When I ring the bell she calls out, 'It's open,' so I walk in and put the sneck down after me.

'I can't get my legs going at all today,' says Mrs Shiner. She's lying on the settee propped up on cushions with a patchwork blanket over her. Her face is the colour of lard.

'You shouldn't leave the door unlocked,' I tell her. 'Anybody could walk in, a serial killer or something.' She smiles sort of vaguely at me. 'I'll make you some tea. I bought some milk on the way here. And I've got you some sweeties, look.'

'Bless you, Becky,' she says, dead quiet and serious like.

There's a couple of foil containers on the kitchen worktop. One says lamb casserole and the other says baked alaska. When I ask, Mrs Shiner says they're from the Meals on Wheels but she's not hungry, she'll eat them later. She can't wait to get going on the story again.

'When he was about eighteen months old, Monty started to get boisterous. He had a mind of his own, he'd do what *he* wanted, and he was very strong. He was into everything, Becky, I needed eyes in the back of my head. All sorts got broken. I smacked him sometimes with a rolled-up newspaper but I don't think he even felt it. He had a way of staring at me with these ... defiant eyes. I couldn't control him, and Edgar - well, he'd never had much truck with him.' She twiddles a hanky and sighs. 'I think Edgar resented the love I gave to Monty. We hadn't been proper man and wife since I'd had the big operation,' she says, in a whisper.

I write down, *'Zero sex'*.

'Lord bless us and save us!' she yells out suddenly. She's doubled up with pain so I prop her up to make her comfy and sit there until her legs stop knacking. When she starts talking again, her breath comes out all puffy.

'We had to hide him, of course. When the rent man came on a Tuesday I used to put Monty in the box room with all his toys and he'd be quiet for a while. But he developed a terrible temper and he used to chatter and squeal like billy-o if he wasn't getting attention.' Mrs Shiner gazes up at the ceiling and her eyes well up with tears. 'I was very upset about what Edgar did. We had some fearsome rows, but at the time I couldn't see any other way. I've never forgiven myself.'

Now she's blarting really bad, her chin all wobbly and tears trickling down her cheeks. I'm not sure what to do. When the crying tails off I take her to the bathroom to get washed and sorted. It takes ages even with her walker because her legs are killing her. She asks if I'll help her into bed. I can't believe how tiny she is, it's like undressing a doll. She's spark out straight away.

Me and Jade go down the park and sit on the swings. We've bought chips and curry sauce from the Tung Wah plus two bottles of Hooch and some tabs. Jade fancies this lad who works in the Blockbuster Video and she wants me to ask him to go out with her.

'Go on, Beck,' she pleads. 'I'd do it for you.'

'No way,' I protest. I'm not gonna be a goosegog and anyway he looks like the ugly one out of Westlife.

'We're supposed to be best mates,' moans Jade. 'You've changed since you've been going to Mad Lucy's. I bet the old witch has put a spell on you or something.'

She's still using her walker but she seems a bit brighter when I visit on the Friday. Mum's given me some Horlicks to give her. When I chuck the carrier in the bin I notice about six Meals on Wheels cartons, they haven't even been opened. She's put a bowl of nuts out on the table. I help myself to a handful while she cracks on with the story.

'Where was I? Oh, yes. Well,' she says, 'Edgar decided Monty would have to live in the loft. He built a wooden ... cage, I suppose you'd call it. It was canny big, but it was still a cage. Monty screamed something terrible for the first couple of days. I expected the neighbours round, but old Mr Thing next door was deaf as a post, thank goodness. I used to sit with Monty in the afternoons, but not for too long because Edgar said it would unsettle him. I used to hold his finger through the bars. It broke my heart to see that look in his eyes. So sad, it was. Sad, and reproachful. Edgar used to see to the feeding, morning and evening, and Monty seemed to calm down after a while.'

I guzzle another handful of nuts.

'After that, I had a bad turn with my legs.

Couldn't move, they'd seized up completely with the rheumatics. I missed sitting with Monty but Edgar saw him twice a day so I had to make do. Then, one day ...' Mrs Shiner pulls out her hanky and her bottom lip starts going. 'One day, I'll never forget it, Edgar came down from the loft and said Monty had passed away. Peacefully, in his sleep, those were his words. He said orang utan years were like twenty of ours, which made Monty nearly seventy, a grand old man. I didn't know any better, not then. Becky, pet, it was the worst day of my life.'

Suddenly she starts blubbing big-time, stuff coming down her nose. I go over and cuddle her. She's such a tiny wee thing, I can feel the bones sticking out in her back. Her arms are like twigs.

It's ages before she stops crying.

'Don't mind me, Becky, my little love,' she says. She blows her nose like a trumpet and settles herself down. 'So anyway, Edgar said he'd take Monty and bury him on Gentleshaw Common, near the Windy Tree where we used to do our courting. I used to say a prayer for Monty every night, but I couldn't bear to live in the house, not after that. The doctor wrote to the council about my legs and they moved us to a ground-floor flat near the Legion Club. We lived there nearly ten years, until Edgar died.'

I can't think of anything to say. I realise I've polished off the nuts.

'Sorry, Mrs Shiner. All the nuts have gone. I never meant to ...'

'It's all right, Becky, pet,' she says. 'They're those ones you brought the other day. I can't chew them with these dentures so I just sucked the chocolate off, it tasted smashing.'

Jeez!

'Anyway,' she continues, 'it wasn't until I was

going through Edgar's things that I found it. A cutting from a newspaper, it was. He'd kept it in a biscuit tin with a load of other rubbish, the sly old bastard, excuse my French.'

'A newspaper cutting? What did it say?'

She takes a deep breath - well, deep for her. 'That Monty's body - it must have been Monty, of course - had been found. I could only see the headline, I hadn't got my specs on, and anyway I couldn't bear to read any more. *Remains of loft ape discovered*, that's what it said.'

'So he hadn't buried him on the Common then?'

Mrs Shiner sniffs. 'No. Left him to rot in that loft. Monty, my poor, poor baby. I even wondered whether Edgar - I told you how jealous he was - I even wondered whether he'd ... Oh, it doesn't bear thinking about, Becky. I could torment myself to death. I'll tell you this much, though. I'll never forgive him, not as long as I draw breath." She raps her fingers on the metal Zimmer, to show she means business. 'I've still got that clipping, I'll look it out for you. And some photos of Monty when he was a baby. I'll have them ready for you next time.'

She seems to perk up then, and there's a wicked twinkle in her eyes.

'I danced on the old sod's grave, you know.'

I clap my hand to my mouth. 'You never? Really? You didn't *sing* as well, by any chance?' Might as well check out Jade's story.

Mrs Shiner grins. 'I most certainly did. " Who's Sorry Now?" That was the song. They all thought I was grief-crazed, but I was determined the give the evil bugger the send-off he deserved. The Full Monty, as I like to think of it. *The Full Monty!*'

And she laughs and laughs for ages, really tickled. The tears start to run down her cheeks and she can hardly get her breath. I'm worried she'll have a heart attack or something but then I start giggling as well and soon we're both at it like a couple of hyenas. I never thought I'd see Mrs Shiner this happy. I lean over and kiss her on the cheek. It feels soft, like velvet bog-paper.

'I can't come on Monday,' I say. 'Mum's taking me to the Metro Centre for some new trainers but I'll see you on Wednesday.'

She squeezes my hand in her little sparrow's one.

'I'll look forward to that, Becky,' she says.

I meet up with Jade in the Upper Crust for a cheese toastie. I've bought some marshmallows for Mrs Shiner to suck while we look through the photos. Jade says she's gone off the lad in Blockbuster since he's had a buzz-cut and she's noticed his ears are like wing-mirrors. I could have told her that.

'I see Mad Lucy's bought it, then,' she says.
'Bought what?'
'*It*. Popped her clogs. The warden found her Sunday morning, sat in her chair. She'd got malnutrition, that's what mum heard. Starved to death. Looked like a skelly. Hey, what's up?'

The cheese tastes like sick in my mouth.
'Beck, where you off to?' Jade yells after me.

I'm out of breath from running when I get to Mrs Shiner's bungalow. A Transit van's driving off. *Wally's Removal's and House Clearence*, it says on the side. There's a puddle of black oil where it was parked. The warden comes out of Mrs Shiner's front door, locks it with a key and walks away like she's in a hurry.

There's nothing left. No curtains. Nothing.
My eyes are stinging. I stick my hands in my

pockets and feel something squidgy. Then I walk up Mrs Shiner's path and lay the bag of marshmallows on the doorstep. There's a lump in my throat the size of a ping-pong ball.

'Remains of 10 ft ape discovered.'
News headline on Teletext.

White Frost On Grass
Wendy Robertson

Brakes screamed for life. Rubber gummed itself to tarmac. Noise invaded my brain: the grind of cars; lions roaring like people; people growling like lions. A girl. There was a girl. Her hand was digging in my shoulder. I could hardly see her through the haze, but I knew from the very scent of her she was young.

What was she saying?

I opened my eyes so wide my eyelids hurt. The stud in the girl's tongue glittered like the morning star; her tongue was red, red as a garden poppy. Her teeth were sharp and gleaming.

She gripped me tight. 'Hey you! Whatcha thinkyer doin'?' Her voice was rough as a puppy's bark. 'Just about bought it then, din'cha?'

'Let go! Let go of me, will you?' I found my voice at last and shouted against the roar of the traffic.

She loosened her grip and I fell back against a wall. 'An'-thank-you-very-much...' Now she was a sulky puppy chanting the words. 'Thank-you-very-much-Anne-Marie-for-saving-me-from-frigging-certain-death.'

Her hand, when I grabbed at it, was remarkably soft. My lips would not stretch properly round the words. 'Sorry... I'm sorry. How d'I get here? One minute the park gates. Then next out here. Cars. Lions. Lorries. Oh dear!' I had to turn quickly to one side so the spewing vomit didn't catch her. My throat burned and my mouth felt filthy.

Then she laughed. Her smile dimmed the glitter of the afternoon sun. 'Lions! Whoops! Been on the pop have we? Here, get hold of my arm. There's bogs at the station. Nice wash and brush up and we won't know the difference.'

The station toilets were empty; she removed my bulky shoulder bag, peeled me out of my coat, ran a basin of water for me and watched while I splashed my face and hair. I rubbed my hands on the stringy roller towel.

She held out my coat. 'There what did I tell yer? Better, innit? Getcha coat back on. I'll button you up. Here's your bag. Now no one'll know the difference.' She hung my bag on my shoulder.

My vision cleared and I took a closer look at her. 'I've seen you before. I know you.'

Probably one of Jake's ex pupils. All sorts they are. All sorts.

'And I seen you. That purple coat with the big bows and the swagger back. Couldn't miss it. Every Friday on the button. That friggin' purple coat.' Her tone told me just how naff my coat was. 'Yeah. I seen you. Give me many a ten pence ancha?' She assumed what was obviously not her own voice. ' *Can yer spare us ten pence for a cup o' tea missis?* Give us ten pence every time, dincha? But only on the way back to the train when...'

I pulled on my gloves. 'When I'm the worse for wear?'

'You said it, not me.'

I loved her now. I loved her hair. I loved her smile. I loved her like she was my own daughter. 'Here, Anne Marie – was that your name? Why can't I take you for a cup of tea now here at the station? We can have a cup of tea together.'

She eyed me narrowly. 'Yer not a dyke are, are yeh?'

I knew the word from the books Jake made me read. 'Nah. Don't be silly.'

'Anyway, I'm wasting time standing here. Could have made a fiver, the time it's taken to clean you up.'

I was desperate now. I wanted her to stay. I didn't want to lose her. 'Look, come for a cup of tea in the buffet here … and I'll give you a fiver. I'm still a bit shaky, you know? '

'We-ell, put like that. But not friggin' coffee. Lager's better. Caffiene's bad for you.'

Here it is. Chaos?

It splits off in shards. It splits off shards of time place and people. It crashes on rock surfaces and shatters again. Crashing. Breaking again.

I was reading all about Chaos Theory, on one of those cards. You know, the ones you collect with that tea that smells of old gardens? I read them all. Card by card. *Rare Roses. Great Composers. Romantic poets. William Blake. The Origin of Species.*

And *Chaos Theory.*

I read a lot now. You know? It started when I was inside prison. Twenty-two hours locked away and you have time to read. True Romance. True Crime. Crime in the Nineteenth Century. All there in the prison library. Some of them smelled funny and looked as though someone had been chewing them.

What else? I read Freud in there, of course. All those cases of funny women. And I really took to old Carl Gustav Jung with his interpretation of dreams. All this is very useful stuff, inside. Plenty of funny women behind bars. And dreams. I prefer Carl Gustav to old Freud, to be honest. Dreams. Dreams. Carl Gustav makes a lot of sense to me.

Like I say I read a lot, but I save my reading for when Jake's out or in bed. Jake's my husband – he was John when I met him. That was before he went on a course called *How To Re-invent Yourself*. Anyway, like I say I save the reading for when he's at work. Not that he's disapproves... well, not of me *reading,* that is. He says it's about time.

He used to tell me for years just how thick he thought I was. Well, he wouldn't use the word *thick*. When we were first married, before even we had Janine, he did this course about Anger Management and learnt that words can be blows. He told me all about it late one night. 'Do you realise, Lilah, that words can be Blows? That it is a violence to Withhold Affection?'

You know what that meant don't you? It meant I had to roll back over in the bed and let him do it again.

Violent? I never saw myself as violent, to be honest. My mother, poor soul, was very violent. But then she was mad. My father was violent too, but that was because he was bad. But me? Mild as mother's bloody milk, I am. Wouldn't say Boo! to a rattlesnake.

No, no. Jake never actually used the word thick. Quite the reverse. He'd be very kind about it, like I was somebody in his Special Needs class. He tells it like this, 'Lilah lost so much school with TB when she was a nipper, you know. No provision, then. No wonder she never caught up, poor soul.'

In those days, he would apologise for me at dinner parties just to show his kind understanding, and how bravely he bore the burden of this unlettered, non-Guardian reading wife. He took a lot of trouble over the dinner parties; set the table the night before, instructed me line by line about the food.

Dinner parties! My mother laughed her head off about those dinner parties. But she's dead of course and can only laugh now in my dreams. Which she does, frequently. At home with her we ate off our knees most of the time, which could be inconvenient. The grease from the chips would seep through the paper and stain your skirt.

Stains on your skirt can be embarrassing in more than one way, you know. The teacher once took me to one side and told me about the stains on my skirt. I bunked off school for three weeks after that because I just couldn't face him as I came through the classroom door.

Well, anyway, you can see why I'd keep all my reading a secret can't you? Jake'd be poking his way into my head, like he used to at the beginning, pushing suitable books on me, raising my consciousness and all that. Those were the books with green covers written by women who had maidservants to bring them tea, while they wrote about the significance of a room of your own. If you were a woman that is.

Some of those books Jake pushed onto me were Janine's, of course. They came highly recommended. She was very clever, my Janine. Top of the nursery, top of the class, top of the college. Biggest earner in her section of the merchant bank.

I had this dream where I tell my mother her granddaughter is a merchant banker dealing in *futures*. 'Futures?' she shrieks in that cackling voice of hers. 'Futures? Well, you tell her that's what comes from having a gypsy for a grandma.'

I woke up laughing at this but never dared to tell Jake about it. He loathed my mother almost more than he loathed Anthony Wedgewood Benn. Tony Benn he is now. He must have gone on that *How to Reinvent Yourself* course, like Jake.

Janine plays the piano. Can you believe it? My daughter? She sings too. Low and throaty like Sarah Vaughan. And looks! Hair like thistledown as a baby, like a new penny when grown. A Daddy's girl, of course, from start to finish. Before she was born he did this course on *How To Raise A Genius*. He used to play tapes to her, chant rhymes into her ear from the day she was born; training her up to greatness, he called it. Always wanted her to be better than anyone around her and she always was.

Janine was *his* from the start: his personal experiment. He chose her games, her friends, her books. He chose her O Levels and A levels. He read all her set books alongside her with every course. He careered round the country with her to sort out just the right university. Five offers! She had her pick. He took all her successes very personally. Seemed to me that he saw the success was his, not hers.

Of course, he drove her to college on that first day: car piled with luggage, heaped with books, plants, kettles. He was almost sick with delight. It was their own special adventure. *Two Go To College.*

She did ask me to go with them. 'Won't you come, Mum? You'll be company for dad, All the way home.'

I was flattered. 'Would you like me to come, Janny?'

Jake exploded. 'No need, no need. We all know your mother has other things to do Janny. In any case you know she cries at the drop of a hat. You wouldn't want her to embarrass you, would you?' Then he laughed that neighing laugh of his, yanked the car door open, swept his baseball cap from his balding head and bowed her inside.

For years those two would natter with each other on the phone about Current Affairs, the Stock Exchange and the very latest books on social issues. They even raced each other to read the whole of the Booker short list and backed their choice of winner at Ladbrokes. Can you credit it?

So, even now after all that's happened, you can see why I keep this reading secret, all to myself, can't you? I hide the books in the back roof space with the bottles and the cigarettes.

Where was I?

Chaos Theory. The screeching traffic. Rubber on tarmac.

I may be wrong, (I am usually wrong: the wrong end of the stick and I are old friends), but as far as I can make out, Chaos Theory says everything is connected, even the most random and chaotic events. I like this idea. I hug it to me. On the market one day I found this book with photographs in it. Computer simulations. Quite breathtaking. Like works of art. See? The camera pulls back and back, see? And what seems to be random specks become swirls, and the swirls become a great design.

Almost makes you believe in God, doesn't it? I couldn't say that to Jake, of course. He's through his Buddhist phase and into Humanism now. Poems over the grave and guitars and all that.

And now I know that good old Carl Gustav has something to say about that as well: God and things. Only connect. Now then, did he say that or was it someone else?

Talk about chaos. The screeching brakes. The almond oil smell of burning rubber is in my nose, invading the threads of my hair.

Her name was Anne Marie, the girl who pulled me to safety out of the way of roaring cars. She had dense black spiky hair and black lines around her eyes. They were bright, those watchful eyes: birdlike and cold.

We didn't say much in the station café. She didn't tell me her life story and I didn't tell her mine. She coughed quite a bit. We peered into our drinks and talked about the weather. The weather!

'Whatcha think about this friggin' rain?' she

said. 'It's rained every day for a week. Wreaks havoc with the graftin. Friggin' rain.'

'It must be hard on you, out in all weathers... ' Christ! I sound like one of those long nosed women Jake gets to come to the dinner parties. 'Do you have a flat or something?'

'Flat? Yer jokin' aren't yer?'

'So you sleep outside, then?'

'So we do. Until the friggin' filth moves us round. It's their pastime, moving us around in the early hours.'

'How do you manage to sleep?'

'Mostly I don't sleep. I stay awake.'

'Stay awake? How do you manage that?

'Well, If I've had a good day I stay awake with a little help from my old friend Whizz.'

'Whizz? Is that your boyfriend?'

She was still laughing when she helped my to buy my ticket and put me on the train. It was only when I got home that I found my purse had been lifted.

The next day I travelled back on the train, sober this time, to find Anne Marie, coughing out her guts on the pavement. I never asked her about the purse, just bundled her back onto the train and brought her home.

Of course Jake didn't like it when I brought Anne Marie home. I heaved her into the sitting room, closed the door behind her, then turned to face him.

'You want that girl to stay here, Lilah? The girl smells. It's a big mistake. I won't have it.' His face was yellow and wrinkled like custard which has stood too long.

Anne Marie didn't smell. Jake always accused people he didn't like of smelling. 'She'll die out there,

Jake. Out in the street. She has pneumonia. Listen to that cough.'

His yellow face flushed with purple, like a bruise. His hands kept curling into fists, then going loose. I wondered if he was remembering those Anger Control seminars. How I wished he would hit me. At least that would be a touch freely offered, without calculation.

It was twenty odd years since he had touched me. It's like he made a hobby of avoiding it. Touching me. I don't know what started that off. Probably Janine. Once he had Janine's hand to hold, once he had her to tickle and to cuddle, he didn't need anyone else. Oh no! I'm not suggesting anything funny, like that child abuse stuff you read about in the papers. Not at all. A daughter was all he needed. Not a wife.

I watched him carefully. 'She can go in Janine's room.'

I could hear his teeth grinding. Then, 'No, I tell you. What has got into you, you stupid woman? There are hospitals. She should go to the hospital.'

'She won't go to hospitals. There's Janine's room, isn't there? She never comes home now.'

'No! I'm telling you no.'

'Just a week or so, Jake, until she feels better.' I keep my voice mild, entirely lacking in defiance.

'No!' he shouted. 'No!' He took a step towards me, his fist curled tight now.

The sitting room door opened and there was Anne Marie hanging off the doorjamb. 'Well!' she gasped, 'Yer didn't tell us yer husband was a wanker, Lilah.'

He turned from me to her, then back to me again. He spluttered 'Oh! Oh!' Then he grabbed his anorak off its specified peg and slammed out of the house.

>   Anne Marie croaked out a laugh then slithered down the doorjamb in a half a faint.
>   'Now, pet,' I said, getting one arm under her arm and round her shoulders. 'Let's get you into bed.'

So there you have it. Jake took that one look at Anne Marie and stayed out of the way. He retired to the little box room he will insist on calling his study. He was permanently yellowish white with anger. I hadn't seen him look so shaken since the billy-goat cornered him on our honeymoon: the highlight of a very dreary holiday for me. We never went back to the countryside for holidays, after that. Jake took to pontificating that the country was very much overrated, as a holiday destination.

After our honeymoon our holidays consisted of Paris alternating with Bruges, year in year out. Paris bleeding Paris. Bruges boring Bruges. You wouldn't think you'd be bored with Paris would you? I can tell you I was so pleased when the Berlin Wall came tumbling down. The riverboats in Budapest and Prague were a bloody marvellous change from those fucking *bateaux mouches*.

Where was I? Oh yes. Jake avoided Anne Marie as though she were a resident tarantula. From the first morning he crept out to work at seven o'clock. Scared stiff of seeing her over the cornflakes. See?

He needn't have worried. It took me three days to get her temperature down and her head off the pillow. You'll be impressed when I say I didn't have a single drink in that time. Motivation, see? I was wary that Jake would come home at some odd hour and throw her out. But luckily he was well into his usual routine of staying after school for meetings, followed by tea in the domestic science department with Miss Flagg, who is a fellow Humanist. Then on Tuesdays he goes on to his Steam Train Society, Wednesdays it's Nineteenth

Century Literature, Thursdays it's his class in Mandarin Chinese.

It was when Anne Marie got up and started moving round the house properly on Saturday that he snapped. Late on the Saturday night I was lying in bed when I heard the telephone downstairs tinkle. I picked up the bedroom phone and earwigged the call.
Jake has called Janine.

'Dad? I haven't got much time. I'm reading up on South American Metals for this meeting tomorrow...

'It's your mother, Janny, she's...'

'Dad? I she ill, is she...?'

It is quite nice to hear the thread of worry in her voice.

'What is it, Dad?' she says.

'Ill? No. Worse than that...'

'Dad!'

'There is a creature...'

'Creature?'

'She brought this creature into the house. I'm afraid your mother's lost it, Janine. We know she's always been, well, ten pence to the pound, poor thing. Look at your grandmother. But this! This is crazy.'

'What is it Dad, this creature? A gerbil? A cat?'

'It's a girl. A street girl?'

'A prostitute?'

'She's probably that as well, I shouldn't wonder. She lives on the street. She has cut marks on her arms and she has – dare I say it – the odour of the street about her.'

There is a rustling at Janine's end. A man's voice, surly and tired, calls, 'Jaye! It's cold! Come to bed!' Then both Jake and I can hear a door click shut.

Jake coughs.

Janine says, 'Now, Daddy, what do you mean she's brought a street girl in?'

'Found the creature begging at King's Cross. Of course I warned her. But she's taken it into her head to rescue this ... thing. It's just too bad. Pathetic. I came home today to find stinking trainers in the hall and...

'D'you mean she's staying there? The creature?'

'Janine.' He pauses. 'She's put the creature in your bedroom...'

Bored, bored with his voice and with hers I crash down the receiver and hope they notice.

On the Monday, with Jake safely at work, Anne Marie came downstairs looking surprisingly perky. Her hair was drawn back in one of Janine's scrunchies and she was wearing a neat tee-shirt and jeans. Jake always insisted that we always keep these in Janine's bottom drawer in case she returns home unexpectedly. I'm not quite sure why we do this. Would she come home naked, do you think? No, it would be Prada or Calvin Klein in leather luggage.

Anyway, apart from the fact that the blackness of her hair was just too dense, Anne Marie might have been anyone's daughter in this ticky-tacky street. They're all made of ticky-tacky and they all look just the same. You know that song?

Anne Marie threw my purse on the kitchen table. 'Yours. You didn't go through my bag?' she said. 'You would have found your purse if you'd done that.'

'It's your bag, pet,' I said. 'I wouldn't go in your bag,'

Plastic shrieked on plastic as she pushed it across the Formica. 'I'da thought you'd be keen to get it.'

I left it where it was. 'Why d'you take it?' I said.

She shrugged. 'Because it was there. Force of habit. Begging. Robbing. It's a way of life.'

I waited for her to tell me something about herself, but she didn't. She never did tell me much about herself. Suddenly she leaned forward over the table and I could see the pale skin under her eyes and the fine down on her cheek. 'Why d'you get together with him? That Jake? He's an ugly bugger. And that friggin' voice! Like a strangled cat. No human being talks like that,' She blinked. 'And you. Well you're not bad looking even now.'

'Bloody good of you,' I said.

'Don't mention it.' And she smiled the mischievous smile of a child. I smiled back her.

'Why?' she persisted. 'Different as chalk and hen's eggs, you two. You even talk different. You talk, well, common, compared with him.'

I stared at her. 'Well, he was an ugly bugger then, Anne Marie, and entirely without charm. No one in their right minds would have him. But then I was the daughter of a mad gypsy who didn't know her arse from her elbow. The two of us had been thrown out of our house. He had a job and I didn't. And he was clever. Always spouting stuff. Seemed harmless enough then. But...'

'But in the house he thinks he's bloody Hitler,' she nodded. 'I've heard him.'

'You've been listening!'

She shrugged. 'Friggin' thin walls, this house.' She looked round. 'Any lager in this *ken*?'

'Just beer.' I hauled some of Jake's bottles of real ale from the pantry, opened a bottle of red wine and placed them on the table. We drank through the morning in quiet companionship. We exchanged the occasional confidence but the best thing was the drink and the company. In one burst of talk she painted a picture for me, of life in care. Seemed like it was some kind of bloody elaborate apprenticeship in the arts of fending off unwanted advances, of robbing and of the use of various substances to soften your view of the world. I told her about my mother who was the daughter of a true Romany and went mad in the end with the confinement of a house. Especially because it was Jake's house. How even in her more rational times my mother would howl to the full moon wailing that living *in brick* was no fate for a true Romany.

'*In brick?*' Anne Marie whistled appreciatively. Then she leaned across the table and took hold of my hand. 'I tell yer what, Lilah, let's have a bit of fun. We'll go down the town and do a bit of grafting.'

Months later the expensive lawyer, hired for me by Janine, tried to make out to the court that it was the red wine that did it. That in my weakness I was led on by a wicked girl to steal all that jewellery: the stuff which was weighing down my pockets when I was arrested. I intervened there and then in the court and told the judge it was the best bloody time I'd had for twenty years. That I had enjoyed myself that day. And that Anne Marie, the girl in question, had none of the goods, none at all, on her. Had she? How did they know it was not I who was leading her astray? I was the grown up after all.

Still, my counsel tried to defend me against myself. So finally I had to shut him up by telling the judge to send the police to search the back loft of my house where they would find the perfume and the razors, the hairdryers and handbags which were my booty from all those years going up and down to London every Friday. I'd been doing it for years. As I said to the judge, in many ways meeting Anne Marie was very nearly the saving of me.

But not quite.

I suppose it was my long history of undiscovered

crime and unrepentant defiance that got me my custodial sentence. Prison was bad but not too bad. Being older gave me grief from some directions. It's hard to call a young woman of twenty five 'Miss', and to jump when spoken to. The odd one of them quite liked to make you jump. My little smile was seen as very offensive. Some of them, I thought, must have had a problem with their own mother. Oddly enough, some the young girls made a bit of a mum of me. It was a strange feeling, one which I'd never experienced with Janine. The regard of these young women was a protection in its own way.

Jake came one visiting day, but I told them I would not see him. For the first time in more than twenty years I could live through twenty-four hours without the constant drip of his presence around me. Despite the bars, the rattle of keys and the smell of disinfectant, I relished such wonderful freedom.

Janine came to see me every month and I swear she seemed more interested in me now than ever she had been. She asked lots of questions about the prison and the women I met there. However I must have been mistaken about her true interest because just before my release she took up a very well paid banking job in Mexico City and we haven't seen or heard from her since.

Anne Marie did try to visit me in jail but was turned away because she didn't have the proper pass. She told me so in a letter, which came with an Israeli postmark. *Then afterwards, Lilah, I went back to your house and tried to talk to buggerlugs about you. Do you know what? He tried it on with me! Hand up the skirt! I socked him where the sun don't shine and that stopped him in his tracks.*

I had a great laugh at that.

I read the letter again later. You do that in

prison. Read your letters again and again. This time I was struck by how very well she wrote. Sharp, very sure of her own voice. I suppose there was a lot about Anne Marie that I never knew.

Best of all, there in prison, I could read what I wanted without it improving my female consciousness. I could plunder the battered library shelves on my own. I could order any book I liked from the librarian, a girl with hair like black rain. That was how I found Freud and Jung, Sylvia Plath and William Blake. There was even a book on the origins of trading in tea in the British Empire. That was a very old book.

Of course Jake was here in the house, waiting for me when I got out. He looks thinner and uglier than ever and has nothing to say to me. He is probably put out about Janine. I don't think his imagination is up to thinking of her alive and breathing, half a world away. As well as this, I think he might be scared. I can't think why.

I sleep in Janine's room and he doesn't challenge my desertion. He's stopped going to all his clubs, all his courses and comes straight home from school. His friend Miss Flagg the domestic science teacher has rung three times but he won't come to the phone. He eats in front of the television and I eat in the kitchen. He is barely visible to me in our everyday life. Perhaps that's why he is frightened: that he will become so transparent, that he is invisible altogether; that he will not only fade from my life but fade from the life of the world as well.

Sometimes, like I say, I hear these crashes and rushing noises. Sometimes I see spangles and stunning cartwheels of light. Sometimes the light becomes solid, breaks off in bright shards and crashes onto the hard kitchen floor. It gets tangled in the cobwebs under the table and between the chairs; it settles on the tufts of grass growing between the tiles. Carl Gustav. Cut glass. Spiky shards. Frost on grass.

It nearly drowns me at times, all this light and sound. But it is all right. From the moment I read those cards on the tea packets and saw the pictures in that book, I knew.

Chaos.

The world has been in chaos since the day I was born. But now I know that chaos melts again into glorious scintillating form and I am safe. I would like to tell all this to Jake as he shuffles round the house but I can't. We don't talk at all now.

I suppose that's just as well, when you think of it.

New Fiction from the North

Tom In A Willow
Anne Spillard

The underside of leaves was all around me. I felt the drag of bark and its sharpness on the bare skin of my thighs, below my shorts. I stayed quite still, my flesh merging into the flesh of this branch, where it had split. It was the lips of this gouge that cut into my skin.

The tree moved all the time. Even in the still evening it shivered and shushed, because it grew strangely tall, forty feet or so above the tasselled rushes, and its branches leaned over the waters of the Frome. The coolness of the river was constantly renewed as the tide crept past to Wareham, creating disquiet and downdraughts where the hot summer air caught at it.

Inside all this movement, I was the eyes of the tree, and I peered downwards into the water. The tree's branches protected me, shifting, weaving camouflaging shadows across my skin, that was browned by summer, and dusted with moss and lichen.

The boats shifted too, tied by their painters to my roots. I could look straight down at them, at their fibreglass bodies painted in eggshell blue. I could wait in anticipation while the rowers clumsily shipped the oars giggling to each other - but quietly, so as not to attract too much attention from the other boats that plied up and down the river.

I waited to see again the act of love.

By now I had learned much of the pattern, for I had seen this act so many times below me, peering, as I knew I should later have to, through the thickening gloaming. At the slow foreplay, such as would go unnoticed by the passing boaters in their various craft; the hand creeping under a blouse's hem, or slipped into a trouser's waist, or slid along the thigh under the fullness of a cotton skirt. The close embrace and desultory conversation that, as the light began to fade, became more urgent and persuasive, till the boat would rock precariously on the mud, wrenching at its painter.

Then I would begin to lower myself through the dark branches, under cover of the gathering hoarseness of love's emotion, or the soft murmurs of unconvincing protest, till I was standing barefoot on my tree's rheumatic fingers, as close as that, so that I could see pale triangles of flesh, the curve of breasts beneath his outspread fingers, the clumsy arrangement of copulating bodies.

For it is not easy to make love in a hired rowing-boat, with its immoveable thwarts. Thwarts, thwarted, athwart the thighs of his beloved, the positions all the more imaginative because of the difficulties to be overcome.

Sometimes lovers would try to leave the boat and scramble onto the bank. But there is only mud, mud and the sharp stalks of the rushes. Then I would slip behind the trunk of my willow, till I could climb to its lower branches, safe again till they retreated, as they had to do, for there was deep marsh and a cutting behind the river bank, to drain the flood at dangerous tides, and there was no place for lovers.

If they had penetrated the reeds they would have found my dinghy. But they never did this, because they didn't know the terrain, and there were warning notices posted along the banks.

I heard the untidy splash of oars that I had learned to listen out for. The boats that tied up at my tree's fingers were seldom propelled by experts. Experts zoomed on past here and disappeared round the sharp bend down-river. Their girlfriends sat in the stern looking bored and trying to admire, steering by word of mouth, confused by left and right, because one looked forward and the other looked back, and these boats were rudderless.

Here came my boat, my fly; for I was a spider hung in the centre of my willow web. A sudden gust of cool air lifted off the river as the tide slid its incoming plates over the warmer current.

'The tide's coming in,' I heard her say.

For a moment the heavy windmill sploosh of the oars was silent, and I could see him sitting there, he was watching her, I knew, although his back was to me.

'How do you know?' he asked her. There was surprise and wonder in his voice, so that I knew he loved her.

And she said, lifting her face, that she could feel it. 'I can hear it too,' she said. And this surprised me, for I had taken all the months of summer to learn it.

He peered down at the water. 'You're right,' he agreed, and this made her laugh, that he had to prove what she said.

The boat drifted round in the current. I felt nauseated, disgusted. For now I could see what I had begun to suspect. William Blake was rowing, his eyes peering ludicrously through his pebble glasses. William Blake, with a girl decked in a frilly blouse, and a wide-brimmed sun hat good enough to go to Ascot. Her skirt frothed around her, white and lacy, and I thought of Miriam in *Sons And Lovers*, dressed in her muslin sprigged with embroidered rosebuds.

William Blake. Usually the boats that moored here carried strangers. It wasn't the same, watching fellow sixth-formers. There was an element of disgust, moral displeasure, almost, that was absent when I watched couples unknown to me. In fact no-one personally known to me had ever stopped here before. True, some faces had been familiar - I had seen them round the town, serving in shops, or waiting in the same bus queue as me. But this was a different sort of familiarity. William Blake had travelled with me throughout my youth. We had joined Infant School the very same day, and just over two months ago we had left school together, that is, we had travelled away on the very same bus, for the very last time.

William Blake's father worked in the same shed as my dad at Marine Inc. He was my dad's foreman.

'You should look after William,' my dad would say. But I never had.

I had thought, that last day at school, that our lives would never be shared again. William Blake was off to Plymouth to read Marine Sciences, under the auspices of British Petroleum, and I was going to Cambridge to read English at Sydney Sussex.

How many times had I seen William Blake, nicknamed Smellie, for Blake's 'ancient feet', blubbing, pinned in a corner, while I stood apart, at the other end of the playground, relieved, yes, relieved at his very existence, for it lifted the weight of victim off my shoulders, which is where I always felt it might have been if it hadn't been for him and his pebble-glasses and his too-mild, too-inoffensive manner.

In the end they had to leave him alone, for we were told he was losing his sight, and any blow to his head might be the last of it, and put aside his need for pebble-glasses for ever more. On its own, this information might not have deterred some, but it came wrapped about with threats of GBH charges, Borstal and so on. In any case, it was around this time that Smellie began to show masterful promise at swimming, which made it possible for him to carve out a little niche of respect for himself.

By the time we were sixth-formers, he was only able to read for an hour at a time, and Special Needs visited every week to teach him braille.

I had no wish to see William Blake fumbling in inexpert apology with the sun girl, the girl of sprigged muslin. I wasn't even curious. I knew too much about him, and I had known him so long, and now I wasn't going to know him any more, which somehow gave me a sort of affinity with him.

He wasn't aware of my concern for him, of course, my certainty that this episode would be a miserable disaster. He was talking more fluently than most of the swains of the willow tree. He was talking about tides, and about bores. I began to plan how I could get out of the tree unseen and slip away into the sunset in my dinghy.

Still he wittered on about neap and spring as if he could talk forever. The girl reached out and touched his hand.

'The pull of gravity,' she said. She pulled him up till he was standing.

'Come and sit next to me,' she invited, and for a moment he stopped in mid-flow as he obligingly settled himself, with more grace than most, beside her.

'You are so clever,' she said. She ran her hand gently down the side of his face, and he turned towards her.

'I love you,' he said.

At that moment I began to shake and tremble, at first thinking that some strange fever must have attacked me. Then I realised it was the willow that was shaking. Its vibrations moved with me as if some great organ was playing, its chords shaking the depths of my stomach. The leaves hissed and whispered. The bough on which I sat seemed to stiffen and tense beneath my buttocks.

They both looked up at this disturbance, laughing, surprised. But the tree bent its branches, giving me my last chance, hiding me in leaves and shadow. 'Go now, go now,' it seemed to breathe, as if peeping on tenderness and gentle love was not permissible. As if only lust and the satisfying of sexual appetite could be spied upon.

'The weather's coming in with the tide,' said the girl. They hugged each other, moving closer together against the hostile shudder of the elements. But the elements were not hostile to them. The sun sank redly below the horizon, the tide moved upstream evenly, and the reeds waved across the marsh in gentle motion. Only the tree seemed hostile, as if resenting me. For the first time it resented my presence.

The girl stayed looking upwards longer than William. She looked straight at me, and I froze to perfect stillness, confident of my camouflage.

'There's someone up there,' she said. 'There's someone hiding in the tree.'

William straightened up, taking his hand away from her, looking at her in surprise Then he looked up into the tree.

'Where?' he asked, and I knew he could never possibly see me.

The girl pointed at me, and the tree shivered again. She couldn't see me. She could not. Paranoid, she was, some sort of neurotic. She was weird, she'd have to be, come to think of it, to let Smellie take her on the river in the first place.

'I can't see anything.'

I stared at him in pure defiance. Just this once more, this one last time, I pleaded with the willow. Don't betray me. Its bough stayed tense beneath me.

How can I go? I asked the willow. I want to go, I do. But now is too humiliating, to scramble down now, while they both watch me; to make some lame excuse to William, who would stand there puzzled, but listening politely. The girl would know. She would know I was looking. Worse, she would know about my loneliness and isolation.

Still she kept on about how she could sense a presence.

Then William put his arm around her and drew her head down onto his shoulder.

'Why are you afraid?' he asked her. 'Why are you afraid of me?'

That made her laugh. As if anyone would ever be afraid of William.

'Of course I'm not,' she said, and as if to prove it, she snuggled down closer to him.

The tree had relented, as if it took one step backwards conceding. Very well, this one last time. For I knew this had to be the last. I breathed out more easily.

So, as the paws of darkness crept up the river, William Blake's paws crept over the white blouse, undoing the first button, the second, the third, the cloth peeled back, and the pale small breasts glimmered below me as he lowered his head to kiss them.

This was the time I would usually begin my descent of the tree, each branch and twig familiar to the grip of my bare feet. But the girl was uneasy. Even in the dusk I could see that she had thrown back her head and her eyes stared upwards. The collusion of the tree, that had been so companionable and comforting to me, could no longer be relied on. So I stayed where I was.

When the girl abandoned her suspicion, it was quite sudden, as if she shrugged her shoulders and thought Who cares? Suppose someone is there? Who cares? Or perhaps she thought William was right, that there was no-one in the tree after all.

It was their first time. They didn't know how to do it. I, with my vicarious experience, heard them in their uncertainty. Yet they were certain they were going to, and they persevered, saying no words, till the water slapped rhythmically against the rocking boat, and I heard her breathing through her mouth, ah, ah. Then Smellie's sobs, 'Oh, Oh, Amanda. I love you.'

I had stayed high up in the tree, honouring its displeasure. But Smellie's triumph was too much for me. I was not going to be the last one left in the playground. I was not.

I pulled up hard on the branch above me and began to swing hand over hand out into the air.

'Filthy swine, Blake. You dirty old man.' I was laughing so much that spittle began to bubble at the corners of my mouth. 'Smellie Willie. Ha.'

'Ahhh.' Water splashed, the boat thumped against the bank. They were jumping out, pulling themselves onto the slime.

'Thomas? Thomas Wray, is that you?'

'Who is it?' she was asking, his Amanda. 'Who's Thomas Wray?' I knew the white shirt would be scarred with mud by now, and stains would mar the firm white flesh.

'Come down here, Thomas Wray.' He stood helpless, hand on the grey-green trunk that was black with darkness.

'You come here,' I yelled.

He clawed at the bark, I could hear the scratch of his fingernails. But I knew he would stay there, that I had nothing to fear from William Blake.

'What's the matter?' she was asking. 'Go up there and fetch him down. Don't let him get away with it. We're not just leaving him there.' Her voice was hot and impatient. 'Go on, go up there and bring him down, the horrible little Peeping Tom.'

But William muttered, shamed as he was usually doomed to be, 'I can't.'

'You can't? What can't you do? Why can't you?'

I knew the answer.

'I'm afraid of heights,' he admitted, and I jeered, safe above him, where I had clambered back to the security of the trunk.

'Come here,' said Amanda, and she said it all calm and quietly, where she was standing, balancing on the fingery roots of my tree.

William went to her, meek as I would have expected.

Her hand was feeling along the trunk of the tree, along its lowest branch.

'Hold me steady,' she commanded

'You can't...'

'Just hold me.'

He did, and she rose up, grasping for the branches above, till she had pulled herself up and stood with her feet on the dried summer lichen. I could see the white of her face peering upwards.

'Come down,' she called to me. But I said nothing, while I waited, thinking she'll never dare, she'll never come as high as this, where the branches begin to bend under your weight unless you stay close to the tapering trunk of the tree.

But she began to climb again, and above her I crouched, believing now that she would reach me, while the black presence of Blake shifted to and fro below us.

'Come on down, Amanda. It's not important. He's harmless, Thomas Wray. Looking, only looking.'

But he was wrong. For hadn't I screamed and shouted at him just now? Hadn't I purged myself of looking, only looking?

What did Amanda want of me? Why did she climb so purposefully up towards me? Still she came on, and I shrank back into my leaves, hearing her sounds, the brush of cloth as it caught on twigs, her indrawn breath as she pulled herself upwards.

Her head rose level with my feet. With one foot I could have pushed her downwards, except that I was blank with inaction, numb as if I had no part in this scene, as if I could stand in the shadow, as always, and let it unroll before me.

'I know you're there,' said Amanda. Her face was the blur of a clouded moon.

'Amanda,' wailed Blake.

But I said nothing at all. Of course she knew I was there, for my feet were inches from her eyes.

Then I knew, as she grasped the branch that I crouched on, and her face rose through the dark to confront me. I knew Amanda would never see me, never. I knew why she loved soft William Blake. I knew where they had met. I knew why they were on the river, why they were both innocent and virginal. And I was shocked into spiked and noxious clouds of jealousy that William Blake, who had so little, had so much more than I had.

Amanda put out her hand towards me. Her head tilted at an unlikely angle.

In the very moment that I realised she was blind, I had tensed myself to spring, to take advantage of her hesitation. Then, as one of her hands splayed outwards to grab me, I leapt past her, and she was fighting to keep her balance as I jostled against her to the outer length of the branch, where the leaves were thicker, to hide me.

The branch was soft and tender, bending with my weight. Enough is enough, my tree said. It was my mother, who despised me for loitering in passageways.

My fingers snatched at the slender leaves,

which came away in my hands , my feet slid down, down with the bending branch, and I began to fall. I heard William scream 'Amanda,' with horrible fear, and the scream got louder, I remember, as I hurtled towards it, torn and scratched as the lower branches rose to meet me.

I landed on my back. Soft mud, which at first I thought was blood, splattered across my face. The breath was punched out of my lungs. I tried to breathe, wondered if I could move, could ever breathe again, could see, could hear, could ever think again. I couldn't breathe, tried to take gulps of air, but my lungs wouldn't accept them. The air was there, all around me, I felt its coolness, but I couldn't make use of it, as if my diaphragm was paralysed for ever.

'Oh, It's you, Thomas Wray.' Said with relief. Then he stepped back to the tree.

'Amanda. Amanda.' The infuriating name, over and over.

A hand touched my face, the first breath rasped meanly into my chest. Not enough. Not enough air. Not enough attention.

It was Amanda who leant over me. But her face was turned towards William.

I tried to get up. Already my ribs felt stiff, my throat was sore and dry, my arms and legs stung with scratches.

'Are you all right?' asked William.

Amanda sat back on her heels. 'He'll live,' she said, which made me want to die, to deflate her satisfaction with being right.

She put her hand on William's arm, feeling along it till she was holding his hand. He stroked her fingers and peered at me.

' You'd better come back with us,' he said, 'In our boat.'

Ours, ours. Above, the tree that had abandoned me stretched umbrella boughs, though one hung limp and broken, high against the satin sky.

They tied my dinghy to the boat, and I huddled in the prow, while they sat side by side, one oar each, and the boat ploughed sluggishly through the water, my weight hindering its balance even though the tide was still not on the ebb.

'Why didn't you just tell us you were there?' Blake asked me.

Then I knew that he had no idea, none at all, that I had waited all summer in the tree, watching, watching. He thought that it was by chance that I was there, that I had chosen the place to hide away in solitude, which he understood.

He thought their love-making was unique; that the boat, the girl, the river and the tree were something only he had thought of.

Perhaps she knew. Yes, she knew. She knew a lot of things that William Blake did not.

Then I knew something else about her. Yes, they were in love, and William's certainty and trust in this hurt me momentarily, even as I sat nursing my bruises in his boat, hating him for my humiliation. I remembered the second of silence after his words 'I can't stand heights,' then her reply, which gathered together all her knowledge of what he was like, his vulnerability, his weaknesses. She knew them all, and for now she overlooked them. Later he would exasperate her and she would leave him. I saw the shaped hollows where her eyes were as she bent forward with her oar, and for one instant I pitied them for the time that was coming to them.

'Well,' said William, because I had not replied to his question. We came to the bridge, where couples leaned over, watching us, 'Now you'll have something to write about. You won't have to borrow it all from D.H.Lawrence.'

It was a gentle reproof, not bitter, and he smiled ruefully as he said it.

At the other side of the bridge, the boat-boy waded in from the landing-place to meet us. He dragged us in with sharp impatient tugs, and threatened them, as he must threaten late arrivals every evening, with the loss of their deposit.

But when Amanda stood up, smiling with apology, and unfolded her white stick, he became silent with embarrassment, and helped us to disembark. He lifted the oars from the boat and carried them away to his shed. Still there were places where other boats had not yet returned.

William said to me, 'We'll give you a hand with the dinghy.'

Because I was limping, and in the streetlights we saw, he and I, that blood was dripping from my fingers.

He turned the dinghy upside down and balanced it on his head. Amanda ducked underneath and helped him, following behind. They were like some nocturnal insect, walking unevenly along the high street, and the crowd, standing with their drinks outside the Black Bear, turned to smile as they passed. I lagged behind, wanting no part of them, yet yearning for their closeness, relishing the power of having a dinghy carried for me by them, because I knew about them, what they had done in the boat.

Presently we reached my house, where no lights shone from the windows above the shop. They put the dinghy down carefully on the pavement outside my door. Outside my mother's door.

William took off his glasses and polished them on his handkerchief.

'We'll be off then,' he said.

'Right then,' I said.

Amanda stepped onto the pavement in front of me. She put out her hand and touched my face with her fingers, just as, earlier, she had touched William's. Seeing her make this gesture, William smiled at her lovingly, for he interpreted the touch as magnanimous forgiveness. The pressure of her fingertips increased, demanding my attention. I pushed my face closer to hers, and only then did she take her hand away.

They began to walk arm in arm down the street. I turned my back on them and tipped the dinghy on its side so that I could get it through the doorway. My mother had promised to take it on the roof-rack when she drove me to Cambridge at the end of the week.

As I closed the door behind me, I heard the fading tap, tap of Amanda's stick along the pavement.

New Fiction from the North

On Double Time
Michael Standen

(a tale of the 1950s)

'Them racing pigeons off at two, mind. It's when they're timed from,' said Mr Rivers and was back through the Sheds to the safety of his bolthole. Even a student - which was how Martin was seen here - challenged Mr Rivers's authority just by existing. His authority resided in watch chain and bowler and bloomed best in his room sheltered by bleary glass from Parkinson Street Railway Goods Depot.

It was Martin's second month on the railways and a faultlessly blue June. Since that day of misgiving when he had been handed a broom along with the traditional instruction to 'rearrange the dust' he'd become attuned to Parkinson Street's gentle bucolic rhythms - shaken now and then by the arrival of goods or a visitation from 'Region'. And though the flooding light made only too plain the futility of any sweeping and cleaning activity in this Victorian acre it brought out the stateliness of its architecture. The grainstores by the defunct canal were Venetian palaces, not that Martin had been to Italy; even the Sheds revealed previously unnoticed iron detail. Here he had earned up to eight pounds a week by doing what small latter-day tasks became available or reading when there was no one much about.

Martin busied himself making a nest of sacks and then extracted his bright new Everyman *Wuthering Heights.* An occasional 'coo' sent his eye to his watch. 'Twenty mins,' he told the pigeons. 'You'll be all right with me.' They were creatures of patience and not at risk of heatstroke. His pigeon-despatching apprenticeship had been with 'Shifter' Blaggers whose name and nature were a Dickensian fit. On some dark principle, Blaggers would wait ten minutes after the official release time before opening the basket with the words,'I'll mek you little bastards work.' Blaggers who had it in for parcels, not only those marked FRAGILE either, had it more in for pigeons and they seemed to know it. Martin turned to Emily Bronte, resolving to think no more of the Sheds, of home, of Ann.

It was Chapter II, page 6 and the narrator was arriving at Wuthering Heights and having dog problems. *"'Wretched inmates!" I ejaculated mentally, "you deserve perpetual isolation from your species for your churlish inhospitality..."'*

'Quite,' murmured Martin to himself and then became successfully engrossed as the sun shone and the birds - sixth sense satisfied - awaited two o'clock in feathery calm.

As he now cycled along the Sunday boulevard, he thought back five days to the pigeons and the pleasure of reading. The wild and drastic matter of *Wuthering Heights* had been a balm and it was hard to imagine ever again entering a book with such luxurious sense of escape. You changed in all sorts of ways all the time but were seldom conscious of it. Then he thought of Bill McKechnie, how would Bill manage without 'the Student' to travel with and translate writing for him? Just as the crateful had got safely aloft, circling twice to assist their abstruse calculations, Mr Rivers, their earthbound leaden equivalent had strutted over (alibi of paper in hand) to announce that Martin and one McKechnie were to go out on daily detachment to Sinderby. Collect passes at the pay office. McKechnie had materialised as Bill, about thirty - thin, black-haired, edgy, doing his best. For most of the working week they had clocked on at Parkinson Street then crossed to the passenger side to travel five little stops and half a dozen tunnels to Sinderby.

Bill's early defences of contempt and respect crumbled when at each station under transparent disguises he would ask if it was Sinderby yet. And each hot day he would raise the window by its strap as soon as the first tunnel was entered, then lower it only to be forced to repeat the process half a minute later at the first black puff of tunnel number two. Every day: 'This it then?' and window up, window down. He could not learn, it seemed. The work at Sinderby was slight, nominal, vague. Only the journeying gave point to their days and Bill once said, 'This is like going off to office work, not it, Martin?' The good thing about Saturday was time and a half but when Mr Rivers stood them by for Sunday at double, well that was old rope with jam on it.

'It's our week, youth.' It was then Martin broke the news that he was cycling over direct from home and not coming on the train. 'Yo can't do that! There's a pass made out,' Bill said. He was terrified and Martin rehearsed him in the special features of entering Sinderby: that particular water tower, that long green cutting. Bill might get out short or else disappear for ever in the Peak District - he'd been his brother's keeper for five whole days: Bill was his own problem. Ann had promised to come over in the afternoon and that would top off the day. Free as the air his bike sped through, he'd save her up. Pigeons and literature were in his mind: Bill would respect pigeons, he was sure. Bill feared Blaggers. Education did not have all the effects claimed for it. Bill and even Blaggers taught you something - survival? But what must the world be like without words to read, labels of all sorts? Bill would be sitting in a sweat of concentration. Bill could count though. Was pulling the window up and down in his honour after all?

Approached by road, Sinderby was just as much a backwater, just as picturesque and economically inexplicable. The mainstay of their working week had been timber in plank which they had offloaded from flat trucks, being careful of splinters; then carried to add criss-cross to piles. A game with very large matchsticks. There were many stacks at Sinderby and mostly quite weathered. Whatever it was which needed them must have been modest and slow in its workings, even by the standards of British Railways. Admittedly Thursday had been Sand, three hours' slogging it from waggon to lorry with the driver, in Bill's words, 'patient as a woman at her third wedding'. Thursday had been tough.

Propping his machine, Martin was in plenty of time to field Bill. Two flatbeds, overnight arrivals, would pace a double-time conscience. He surveyed the domain soon to be shimmered in heat. It was like a bit of fifty years ago, a trapped morsel of Edwardian summers. Sinderby was a picnic all right and, treated with the respect due to dead trees and important items like knees and backs, the planks should quietly occupy the time until three, with Ann to follow at 3.10. It was truly more idyllic than any day before the First War. Sand could not possibly show up on Sunday and with not even a Mr Rivers around, Sinderby was an island in the sun.

On time, the tank engine emerged from the cutting and halted, clinking to itself by the half-dismantled passenger arrangements. The only possible traveller had alighted under his own steam. It was Bill, transformed as if in support of Martin's historical musing. He had a suit of good black cloth, shirt with studs, maroon tie; he had waistcoat and watch-chain. The local then departed, juddering a few black snorts into the crystal air. Martin knew to pass no comment on Bill's attire. 'Wood,' he said, 'as per usual.' They stepped across both burnished and rusting rails in professional immunity from cast-iron threats of forty shilling fines.

Then Bill pointed out a waggon he'd not noticed, a refrigerated van announcing itself in fresh paint as coming from Grimsby.

'What's that then?' Bill couldn't read a word on Sundays either.

'Frozen fish.'

'What's fish doin on a Sunday?'

'Left-overs from Friday.' Bill believed him like a kid.

'Bleddy hot for it.'

Martin did want to ask him about the suit. It must just be Bill's way of life. Sunday working had faced him with a choice and he had found Sunday the bigger pull.

Two and a half hours later much of the wood had been stacked. The sun was approaching its zenith of attack and the jacket had gone, carefully folded, then placed on a dusty piece of hardboard. Waistcoat and tie remained; armpits had darkened. Stripped to the waist himself, Martin had the sort of feelings a first sighting in Europe might produce in the ornithologist. Mostly he approved. Whatever the tradition was, it was grandly beyond utility and Bill suffered for it without comment. When it came to 'snap' the bread was parched. They filled their mouths from the standing tap to help the sandwiches down. After many swallowed gulps Bill spat water. 'Railway piss!' he said before fumbling out the all-purpose adjective. Martin sat on the metals in something verging on judgement. He'd travelled with Bill, shared time with him, did not know what to make of him. At any given moment sunlight, time, yourself could press you into something stamped and flat and not to be believed in.

'Not sodding right,' Bill concluded, then, more

philosophically: 'Bleddy isn't.'

'Easy be through by half two.'

'Yo'll get piles,' Bill said - an observation rather than a warning. Martin stood up. 'Who's it you say's coming?'

'Girl-friend. Ann. Due at 3.10.'

'Bit of talk on about a strike -ASLEF like.'

'You ever hear of a strike on Sunday?'

Bill chewed that over. He was always secretive about his snap, conveying it directly from paper to mouth as if it were not for public scrutiny. If wife or mother had prepared it for him, Martin had no idea which. 'She regular then?'

Martin was shying small bits of clinker at a distant oil-drum and scoring about two hits from three throws, being careful to make no omens. She loves me/she loves me not. He knew she loved him. 'I've got the army to do, or raff - probably not the navy.'

'Oh aye,' said Bill.

'Or "aye-aye" - or God Almighty.' Was taking the Lord's name in vain offensive on His day? Bill gave no sign.

'She just a bit of cunt like?'

Bill could help neither suit nor language: it was Sunday and he was at work. 'That's not how I'd put it.'

'That's *where* you put it.' Bill's dark features cackled briefly; it was his first known essay at humour and the first time he had done much at all with his face. Martin was put out. 'Come on, Plato,' he said.

One either end, lift, mind the step down, walk thirty yards, turn it, add it to the stack. The cutting shimmered and Sinderby was silent, digesting its dinner. A barking dog, someone shooting, a frolicsome shriek: Sinderby breaking every commandment perhaps. These few sounds in counterpoint to the crunching tread of their feet and the reverberating clump of the plank going down.

It was done and now the flatbed trucks held no interest. During the night they would be shunted off and others brought: someone somewhere, Mr Rivers perhaps, saw to the ordering of these things. They were each £2.8s.6d better off.

'Yo'll be walking your tart. Here.' Bill produced a timetable kept scrupulously neat. 'Nivver bother with such fiddly stuff.' Martin found that the best afternoon train going back into the city was at 3.13. 'Must be timed to cross here out of the section, with Ann's train,' said he, observer enough to pick up bits of jargon.

'Get an eyeful of what yo nest on,' said Bill pleasantly.

They returned to lunchtime perches, Martin first retrieving his shirt. Twenty minutes to inspect the growth of weeds between the tracks. The sun crammed the cutting and the hollow of Sinderby's railhead, if that was the term, brewing such heat that Martin draped his shirt Arab-style as drops luxuriously ant-trekked down his naked back. Bill had resumed his jacket, not well brushed down.

Ann would have been revising for her exams to the last minute. Martin knew her address, had cycled down her street but with ill grandmother and ill-disposed step-father he'd not been asked into number twelve. She had come three times in all to his house, met everyone: mother and Bob first time, both parents the second. They'd liked her; she them. Successful social intercourse. Father had been skittish and already on the second occasion he could sense maternal trying-on of in-law mantle for size. On the third occasion a month ago the family had been in Birmingham. It was his nightshift week and they had gone into his still warm bed. Despite the heat, a cool shiver squalled his back. Naked with her, he knew and did not know Ann Vaughan. He was as ignorant of her domestic world as he was of Bill McKechnie's. She was Ann Vaughan, autonomous being and not a slice of Lady of Shallott tart. With 3 p.m. approaching, he felt a little nervous. 'Wants a minute to,' Bill declared and they set off for the half derelict platforms. Being late was amongst Bill's many dreads and a quarter of an hour spare was cutting it fine even in timeless sunlit Sinderby where the arrival of anything was more a matter of faith than probability. Next week would see them both back on the Sheds, and Bill to him no more than a distant figure in their twilight. He was more likely to remember Bill than Bill him. The bright cameo was now almost where it belonged, in the past.

Ann came in a bright new diesel, stepping down as fresh as paint herself. Bill had stayed at his elbow and Martin had an ember of concern lest he boarded the diesel and was whisked off into the illegible country. Bill was here on the wrong platform out of curiosity, leaving the only possible thing to do - what his dad had annoyingly demanded on that second visit - 'Do the honours, son.'

She had on a plain white dress and, seeing him in the sun-dazzle, she sent out a wide smile saying 'love'.

'Miss Vaughan, Ann. This is Bill McKechnie, fellow wage-slave.'

'How do you do?' Ann held out her hand and Bill, having wiped his on his thigh, responded. White dress, black suit (equally appropriate for doing honours) shook hands. Dressed for cycling and planks, Martin regarded the Beauty and the Beast slabs of his world, though Bill was perfectly presentable when it came to it.

'Wor your mam a Greenwell?'
'Yes! How did you know?'
'Set of the eyes is Agnes to a tee.'

Bill's smutty old train clattered in and with a

wave he lightly vaulted to the track vacated by the diesel and got aboard. His exit was perhaps done with a style to impress the shining girl. 'He's very nice,' she said.

'Suppose he's OK. Got the train all right?'
'Oh, yes. It was very swish.'
'I sometimes feel like a leech.'
'A doctor?'
'No, silly.'
'Not one of those horrid sucking things?'
'One of them,' he heavily said.

'But whatever for?' No one could do surprise like Ann unless that too was the set of her eyes. He'd been going to make some point about feeding on the dying body of British Railways but the notion contained more in it than he wished to explore. Her question hung, dissipating into the sunshine.

The station yard was divided off from civil Sinderby by a very wide five-barred gate, recently repainted white but dropped from its hinges. Where a colony of plants had established itself on clinker shard the painter had skipped his work. The bike would be safe padlocked and the very last train to town was not until 5.45.

'We could walk down to the river,' he suggested.
'Yes.'
'It's this way I think.'
'I've revised rivers,' she said.
'Tell me when we find it then.'

They ascended a main street fashioned through two or three rural centuries. Brushed by the motoring age it was sleeping it off and - if boarded-up cottages and the odd FOR SALE sign meant anything - would wake to some new Monday morning by and by.

'It's very pretty here,' said Ann. At the highest point they passed the church and then down the other side. 'Early settlements were usually put on hills,' she said experimentally.

'Were they?' He sensed how unsatisfactory he was being but hardly knew why. They had not touched and he felt inhibited and debarred for no reason at all with Sinderby ideal, empty, theirs. She was summer-lovely, honeyed by the sun and with just the right number of freckles. Miserably, sentimentally, he thought of new-baked bread. He asked about exams and was told dates and papers. Hard to imagine himself back in that jungle again. She asked him about the family and was given a shallow account, a skim.

Between Sinderby and the river lay great fields which - just slabs of country - must have been known by generations like the backs of their hands, literally too, for you could still see the ridge and furrow of the common field. Trees kindled by the season, full and motionless, seemed hung down and descending in this light rather than rooted and upreaching. You began to sense where the river was, the line of it. When they had reached its banks he would speak, act, make things real for them and not vague and snagged in moody palls. Reality existed under the circumstance of things but you had to dig it up.

'It's like a painting,' said Ann. 'Only that may be because so many painters paint rivers.'

'These days they just paint the town red.' They were still well short of the river but he stopped. They were facing each other at last. 'I'm sorry, why do I make these stupid remarks to you of all people?'

She considered that as she always considered his words, but it could not always have been for the sense in them. 'Perhaps I'm boring for you.'

'Silly!' A small step and he held her. Her arms craned up behind his head and the shoulderbag swinging. His lips could graze forever on a face like hers but he had nuzzled himself into position to see his watch. They reached the river, arms around each other's waists. This river was known even in London and though now reduced to light frontier duties for County Councils and suchlike, had created real divisions in its time. Celt had disagreed with Celt over disagreeable deities; Saxon and Dane had jumped up and down on its banks; groups of all kinds had been outraged at the presence and proximity of other and usually quite similar groups. Neighbours. It resembled many garden fences and walls across which from time to time things have been righteously hurled.

Though June and summer-dry, its flow was strong in muscular ripples and nervy swirls. One or two lone fishermen had been dabbed in to complete the scene but there was neither house nor bridge in sight. All was massive, elemental, strong.

They walked along a good path. 'I remember my first school song,' he said. 'How about that?'

'"Ba-ba Blacksheep"?'

'No, dopey, the song at my first school. I have been widely and thoroughly educated, I have.'

'Ours is Latin,' said Ann, 'and I don't know it and you can search me what it's about.'

'They're essentially male,' he explained. 'Girls would be more difficult.'

'Girls are very straightforward.'

'Not girls as such. I meant songs for girls' schools. Nothing demeaning at all, rather the opposite. Such things are essentially silly - sillier when it's girls. Now don't go telling me girls aren't silly!'

'They can be,' said Ann.

'Bless her. What do you mean by that?'

'They can have silly ambitions.'

'Doing things like...I don't know...flying jets?'

'That wouldn't be silly if they wanted to,' she

said.

As if on cue, a low-flying jet tore a strip off the peaceful blue day. 'There you are, a DeHavilland Vampire sucking up the taxpayers' money. Could be a girl flying it.'

'There was Amy Johnson who came from Hull.'

'Didn't she disappear? They usually did. Want to sit down?'

'If you do.'

Martin led the way off the riverside path. Courtship was collusion. He strode ahead. There was always this pretence to rest young bones, shelter from imagined draughts and rain in doorways. Demanding ancients were never half so mardy with their creature comfort needs. The littoral was not rich in shelter or cover except for its size and emptiness. Heathy grass waste spread wide up to the tended fields. At last though he found a hollow, a bit dusty, containing a beer bottle and a vole's back door. 'This seems more sheltered.'

She had followed without question. He cursed himself for not borrowing Bobby's camera, not placing himself at his little brother's feet to learn apertures. She was wonderfully worth Kodak capture and her dress outdazzled Unilever. 'Bit mucky I'm afraid.' He removed his shirt and spread it. 'Sir Walter was an ancestor, so 'tis rumoured.' She laughed and dabbed a finger on his nose. She was always eloquent in her looks and touchings as his clumsiness never was. They occupied their hollow.

They kissed and his hand which had circled her ankle expanded slowly over the satisfaction of her calf. Came a point where she drew back a fraction. 'What?'

'It's only...'

'Fishermen go into self-hypnosis. There's no one else.'

'Not them.'

'What then?'

'You know,' she said.

'I don't, love. It was thirty days ago, I've counted. It was OK then.'

'Yes.'

'You don't want to?'

'You know I do.' He took that to be sufficient. Fastenings of hook and loop he managed with precision. She helped him in removing her dress, undoing the last serious obstacle of her bra. He divested himself unaided. She submitted warmly enough if not entirely happily which he knew until the final act of love absolved him momentarily from consequence. She clung to him and her tight-shut eyes were almost like stitched wounds. Yet she held him, it was not dire. Licking her lids he tasted her salinity. 'Come on, sweetheart, the Sinderby Watch Committee starts its Sunday prowl about now.'

Clothing was not the same getting on as out of but she let him see to the little hooks and delved out a comb. Impossible to know what she had made of it. She was flustered not in a way he could mend though he busied himself. Walking slowly back Ann was almost somehow apologetic but also contained - unrealised. He talked of his future, National Service - unknown years stretching earth-brown or sky-blue, the elemental colours of a deathly two years. She listened to what he knew was little more than self-centred raving; he wished to be serious, not humour her. Ann's unknown being, unknown to her perhaps. Violated perhaps. Only their hands joined now. This landscape, this rolling stream oppressed you with its one-way flatness: mindless and horizontal and river-bodged. The fishermen were still transfixed. The rolling stream which got everybody in the end.

Perhaps Ann was simply straightforward. Or he

so crooked he could no longer see it. It was somehow no moral, metaphysical or other sort of question. You could do so much, that was all. Then strength ran out. Desert or icecap got you. Finger or toehold failed. You parched, you froze, you fell. Near the spot of earlier where they had kissed Ann stopped.

'What's up?'

She stood, dangling her shoulderbag. 'Nothing.'

'I'm not stupid for God's sake! There you are as if you had nothing to do with it, with me, with anything else.'

She wept without much noise, neither moving nor dabbing.

'And now this! Please.' He held her and she minimally permitted comforting. Again he licked tears. 'Come on, love, Sinderby's only a little place. It can't take much more of this.'

She let him shoulder her bag and place an arm. They walked towards the church. In the zenith was night's very first touch to the unfailing cloudless blue. 'The trouble with love,' he said, 'is that it's so bloody nerve-wracking.'

'You deserve someone better,' she said.

'Not possible. It was all my fault. Right off, as they say. Something to do with old Bill got me off on the wrong foot. Don't know what really. Funny about him recognising you.'

'Not funny.'

'Tragic then! What about your mother? You've not said much - let alone that she is beautiful as well.'

'I'll tell you about her some day.'

'What do you mean? There's no time like the present. There is no time but the present, *pace* Albert E.'

Ann put up a hand to overlay his which was cusping a shoulder. 'For the past three years she's been

in Rampton.'
'That's the local lunatic asylum, isn't it?'
'That's where she is.'

The Intruder
Margaret Wilkinson

It was summertime in the North-East of England. The room was small and I hunched my shoulders as I walked in. There was a fire blazing in a cute little fireplace. I stood right in front of it burning my face and my knees. The backs of my legs however remained cold.

Fire amazed me. It stirred me. For a moment I got nervous of what might still be inside me, hissing and bursting - and I jumped away. The smell of burning coal was deep and intriguing, but no one else seemed to notice it, reminding me, as if I needed reminding, that I was an outsider here. Yikes! I thought. My mother-in-law, Mrs Abbot, a woman I hardly knew and certainly didn't understand was making me lunch. I felt humble and grateful and anxious and scared. I'd had such a close shave.

Nearly a spinster, I was thirty years old when her son, Colin, plucked me off the shelf. Frankly I'd already given up. There were no suitable men in New York City where I'd lived before I met Colin. Only morons and married men. The Second World War had unbalanced people. They rushed into marriage. Somehow I missed the boat. By twenty-five, I was already an old maid. Men appreciated me, but they were all spoken for - and a girl like me got lonely sometimes. After a while I developed a bad reputation for French kissing on couches. Mister Right was always a snake.

Once I started dating Colin, I decided I was going to play this one differently. I got wise to myself.

When we first kissed, I kept my lips carefully closed like an angel. We got married in New York City. Then he brought me home to England. The Northeast of England had nothing to do with my image of England. I'd expected something else. Still I was grateful. I felt the whole nation had somehow saved me from spinsterhood. The war had been over for eleven years but there was barbed wire on the beaches and concrete bunkers further inland. The streets were bleak and dark. The shops were bare. I was pretty sure they didn't have mambo lessons or maraschino cherries here. There were still shortages. I couldn't buy the things I was used to having. Nevertheless I'd had a close escape and I was determined to make a go of it in England as a respectable married woman.

I sat on the couch taking up too much space with my long arms. Even though I wasn't that tall, my legs protruded deep into the centre of the room. I crossed one leg over the other in order to make it look shorter, then I took a deep breath. My mother-in-law perched like a bird in a winged armchair at my side. We'd been introduced for the first time at her husband's funeral. On other occasions, we'd always been accompanied by Colin. I'd never actually been alone with her before. Colin seemed to think we could be friends. He didn't know I'd sniffed cocaine and danced on a table in Harlem before we met. During the war, Colin's mother had worked in a munitions factory. "Get her to tell you about that," Colin suggested as I was about to set off that morning. "It's a scream. Don't let her bend your ear about spirits though. She's daft for spirits."

"Gan canny," he said when he left me at the bus stop on his way to work. In New York he never used such expressions. But now Colin was home. "Gan canny," I said to myself over and over again on the bus to Mrs Abbot's house.

The couch was called a 'settee.' It was covered in pink cabbages with a ruffle to the floor. I ran my fingertips over the material. I once had had a dress that felt as shiny smooth, but not as stiff. On the tiled mantelpiece there was a carriage clock, a china shepherdess with a broken crook, a framed photograph, a glass ball on a stand, a plate bearing the message - 'Greetings from Whitley Bay,' and a china horse. I looked at everything with a wild lack of focus. When Mrs Abbot was out of the room, I got to my feet, flowing up from my chair, and walked around. When no one was watching, I moved with a languid grace. Frankly, I didn't want anyone in England to know I had a sexy walk. In front of the mantelpiece, I stopped. I picked up the china horse, and felt its hollow belly. Bending my face close, I inhaled its dappled smoky odour. I stood on a silver scorch mark on the fireside mat. These things were so strange, they excited me. In one corner of the room, a dark cupboard with double doors was shut up tight. The wallpaper, a dense leafy pattern of twisting vines, made the room appear even smaller - like a dwelling underground. I focused my eyes sharp as needles and squeezed my hands together - but I couldn't understand what was what.

Mr Abbot's eyeglasses still rested on a small table beside the detective novel he'd been reading when he died. In the lenses, the tips of flames, reflected from the fire, danced. His final illness had been long and hard. The framed photograph on the mantelpiece, I assumed, was of him. He had a bland expression, arched brows and long ear lobes. A more recent snapshot, tucked in the corner of the framed one, showed a little wrinkled man, his face dark with emphysema. I thought of the things Colin had said about his father and shuddered. A gnarled wooden stick I'd seen hanging in the hall when I entered had once been his. His coarse hat was laid on a shelf, half-hiding a shiny wooden board made by Ouija.

One thing I didn't want to do, was catch myself in the mirror over the mantelpiece. If I could see the expression on my face, the eager flame of something still burning, after all my efforts, I thought I might die.

My eyes flitted from the dark cupboard to the ruffled settee. Was there a secret passage? Every English house had a secret passage, I believed. For a moment, I felt like I was not alone. I jerked around. Then I told myself I was being foolish. From the kitchen came the sound of a spoon scraping the inside of a pot.

Under the window, a much polished radio in a large piece of furniture was switched on, and when Mrs Abbot came back into the sitting room, we tried to talk above the murmur of another speaker, and the ping of a tennis ball in a place called, 'Wimbleton.'

"How're ya keeping Hinny?" she asked, a piercing sweetness in her voice. "Alreet?"
"Fine," I told her. I sat down again and re-crossed my legs arranging my skirt over my knees.

Mrs Abbot took little darting glances at me and shrank back. She was wearing a thin cotton dress with a black band sewn to her sleeve and carpet slippers. In her pocket was the dust cloth she used to polish the woodwork.

I held my breath with wonder and delight. This was all so new to me. Nervously I touched my skirt. I had nothing to talk to her about except my surprise and perplexity at English life which made me sound stupid. Or so I thought. Watch your mouth, I told myself. I censored everything I said, not wanting to reveal anything about my former life. If I had wanted to open up, I could have told her plenty. I knew all about swizzle sticks, barflies, strip joints, knockout drops, bug spray, murphy beds, shyster lawyers, cocktail bars, meeting men and cutting loose. But those gritty days were locked up inside me. So I sat there with nothing to say. I was torn between protecting my secrets and trying to develop a relationship with her. I wanted to sound interesting. I also wanted her to like me.

My own mother had given up on me years ago, when I first started going with married men. I snagged a lot of no good married men in the old days. Men with big ugly whiskers, slippery men, heavy breathers, big feeders, men with unusual appetites, guys with street-sweepers and other loud types of shoes on their feet. I held them against me, flapping and twisting. I felt their long slow tremblings. I'd been around the block, as they say. At one time, I was a fireball - but I retained a picture in my mind of something more refined.

"We saw some nice houses last week," I said, self-consciously. Whenever I said anything in the North of England, my voice seemed to boom like a hammer. Was my hair all right? Even my hair seemed too big here - too looping and long. I could look sexy and exotic, like an actress. But I'd left my lipstick and pancake makeup in New York City in my determination to unhook myself from the past. Now I looked sallow. The cold seeped into my scalp. I used to have a great deal of bodily warmth.

"Aye a real place of your own pet. Happy days," she said. But her face looked shut down.

Colin and I were still living in a temporary, but dreary rented room. There were cracks in the walls and one actual hole. The only window looked out on a front garden that had been concreted over. Sheets of newspaper blew against the old gate. Everywhere there was wind. From the centre of the ceiling in our one room, a naked bulb swayed in a mean draught. Living like this with Colin made me feel heroic. I constantly thought about what my family back in New York would say. I was alone out here. I felt a peculiar satisfaction when I considered my situation. My family could go fly a kite.

During the lean and lonely years in New York City, my sisters had avoided and ignored me. An unmarried woman was bad luck. Now I was lucky again, I'd landed a husband like a fish. I got letters from them marked with crosses for kisses, which I didn't answer.

"I remember when we first moved in here," Mrs Abbot said. "Right away I made a clippy mat." I nodded like I understood. Talking to her was a struggle. I tried to guess what she meant. "The garden was clarty. We had a nettie in the back. I fetched drinking water from a stand pipe, and took the bairns' clothes to the wash house."

I gazed at her thin arms and my heart emptied out. She was as tiny as a handkerchief - such a small woman, her eyes meek and lost behind rimless spectacles. I imagined the dead weight of wet clothes. She must have been stronger than she looked. I remembered Colin saying his father was cruel and mean with money. A working man his whole life, he was too tired to come home and be decent. I thought about the gnarled stick that hung in the hall. It had thick knots along its length.

"I'm sorry about Mr Abbot," I said, feeling I had to acknowledge her recent loss. "I wish I could have met him."

"My husband was a wonderful man," she replied severely. "He never asked for nowt."

I nodded stupidly. According to Colin, she'd walked in his shadow.

"I can't believe he's gone." She looked around. "It's like he's still here."

I half expected her to kiss his faded

photograph, but we were not in New York City where people did showy dramatic things for effect.

Colin told me he used to knock her around. Once he broke her ribs. This could be a new start for her as well, I thought.

"He was my rock," she said. "He had a temper, mind. All that shouting. He wasn't a peaceful man."

I nodded again. I'd known all sorts of men.

"Not restful like. Something was always irritating him. He couldn't sit still. Aye, he had his funny ways. Like now, if he were here, he'd be getting irritated about his dinner. His meal had to be on the table sharp."

What did she mean, sharp? I thought about the prickly man, his thorny walking stick that looked like it had been cut right off a tree, and winced.

"Nothing's changed. His things are still here," she continued in a hushed tone of voice. "I kept everything the way he left it." She sighed deeply. "They watch over us you know."

I didn't have any idea of what to say to that.

"You're kidding me," I piped. She was fascinated with the way I spoke out of the corner of my mouth. "Do all Americans do that?"

We must have sat there a long time. I was unused to sitting silently with another person. My own mother, when I saw her, was always yelling at me. I was about to speak, but the silence was somehow pleasant. I gazed at the fire Mrs Abbot had built in awe. Her house was the warmest place I'd been since arriving in England. When the flames began to flicker and dim, she got stiffly to her feet and threw a bucket of coal, that had been standing on the hearth, into the grate. Sparks sputtered in the air and jumped onto the mat. My mother-in-law can do that! I marvelled. It seemed like a big thing to me. She got fuel free from Mr Abbot's former employer - the nationalised Coal Board. Otherwise she wouldn't have had a fire in summer at all. With a whoosh, new flames vaulted up the chimney. I held onto my hat, as New Yorkers would say.

Mrs Abbot found a brown bottle of aspirin, left by Mr Abbot, and took two with an unfinished cup of tea. She had a headache starting. Without speaking, we watched the flames inside the fireplace. It was better than TV, which my mother-in-law didn't have as yet. She was looking forward to Colin buying her a new, 1956 television soon. Colin went to dental school on a scholarship. As I thought about his potential earning power, the room turned gold. The sequins on my cardigan caught the light.

The kitchen was full of steam. On the stove, boiling pans of vegetables caused the windows to mist. This was more like it - my dream of foggy England. I could barely see. "Open the back door," Mrs Abbot shouted from a crouched position in front of the oven, her eyeglasses clouding. In the kitchen she seemed agile, her fingers were as fast as light. The kitchen was her domain. Bending close to check the dinner, she looked like a young girl, hair wisping against the back of her neck.

Through the steam, I staggered towards the place I knew the back door to be and wrenched it open. It was July, cold wet air rushed into the room. I stood for a moment, touching the smooth door handle - gazing out into a brick yard. Surprisingly, I smelled the sea. I stuck my head out. High above, a white bird soared on a current of windy air. Trees could be glimpsed beyond a brick wall. When I turned back to the kitchen some of the steam had already dispersed and I could see more clearly. The table was set with drinking glasses polished clean on the skirt of Mrs Abbot's apron. I offered to help, but she was so able and knew so well where everything was kept, that I just got in the way. I felt big and hulking as I stood in the corner. It was twelve noon, dinner time in the Northeast of England, and everywhere there was an echoing quiet. New York was never quiet. The yelling, jeering and joking, the cars backfiring, the very life of it returned vividly to me.

Only once had I experienced this kind of silence in New York City. A married man, naturally - a real loser named Ernie - took me for a picnic on an island in the East River, drawing me into romance.

We hiked over a footbridge. It was a long walk and I was wearing impractical shoes. We brought a chicken and necked in the grass. It was so still and green, I felt at peace. Then suddenly a loud scream pierced the silence. A long horrible violent scream that made the air around us move. That jerk Ernie had taken me to the grounds of The Manhattan Psychiatric Centre on Ward's Island. He was a real dope. I'd fallen hopelessly in love with him, but I wouldn't allow myself to think about him any more. I'd flushed years down the toilet with no-good men. Instead I thought about my husband Colin's kind features, his slack and slightly goofy face, his tall, bony frame and big feet.

Mrs Abbot and I were having hotpot at a table pressed into one corner of the room. My stomach jumped. I knew I would have to clean my plate. If I didn't, my mother-in-law would misunderstand. For a moment, I remembered hot meatball heroes. It broke me. Stupid with unhappiness, I jammed myself into my seat, my back against a dresser.

"Mr Abbot always liked hotpot," Mrs Abbot announced. On her own, she forgot to eat. "No matter what people say about him now," she continued in a sombre voice, "Mr Abbot always provided. He was a good worker." She looked at me for a moment, her eyes filled with motherly concern. "Marguerite," she asked intently, "do you believe in the other world?"

"I don't know," I said.

The food in England was nothing to dwell on. I spread myself stiffly against the dresser while we ate. "Forgive me hinny, if I've said too much." Mrs Abbot seemed flustered. She had very formal and elaborate table manners. She chewed quietly but after a while her cheeks became red from the heat and the food. She wore an apron, called a pinny, that was smeared and sticky. I wanted to be just like her. If she had any curiosity about me, or my family, she didn't let on. She knew my maiden name had been Hlox. "Was that an American name?" she mused. It was the closest she'd ever come to talking with me about my family, or background.

"No," I told her, "Hungarian."

"I'm certain we've met before."

"At Mr Abbot's funeral," I reminded her, "and a few times with Colin."

"No, before that," she insisted.

After the meal and a pudding of tinned fruit and custard, we made our way back into the front room and sat down again. Mrs Abbot opened her top button for coolness and fanned herself. She pronounced it, 'roasting,' and left the door gaping. The room felt awkward with the door like that. My eyes kept being pulled into the dim draughty hall where Mr Abbot's stick still hung on its own, apart from the coats, hats and umbrellas that were jumbled together on crowded hooks beside it. If a place could be said to be haunted - that hall was it.

From a roll of paper she kept in a drawer, Mrs Abbot took out a single sheet and showed me something she called an automatic painting she'd done in a trance. It pictured two figures in a storm. One of the figures had piercing eyes. "I had the strangest dream about you," she intoned in a voice unlike her own. "Dreams tell me things before they happen. Perhaps you're needed here, lass," she added mysteriously. "Or maybe I'm daft."

I only had erotic dreams. So I said nothing. Half an hour passed. We couldn't seem to get the flow of conversation started again.

Mrs Abbot lit a cigarette with a slender match. I watched as it was lifted from a tiny sliding box, unlike the matchbooks we used at home. 'Matchbooks,' I said the word to myself. The term already sounded odd. When she offered me her pack of Embassy Regals, I declined. I'd given up since coming to England. My mother-in-law's eyes were permanently pink-rimmed from smoke. She puffed avidly, like barflies I'd known, which didn't surprise me. Nothing surprised me any more. I was a woman of the world. But I felt like a little girl.

"Your mam must miss you," my mother-in-law said. She left the room and came back some time later carrying a tray lined with a cloth. Cups, saucers, a teapot, a milk jug and a sugar bowl were arranged on top. She'd brought a cup for Mr Abbot too, I noticed, but of course I said nothing. It must have been a habit that was hard to break.

"Would you get the biscuits love?"

I jumped to my feet grateful to be needed. In two steps I crossed the room. Alone in the kitchen, I took a moment to look around. There was no fridge. In the dim pantry, mooching through the bought biscuits and condensed milk, I felt excited and doomed. A stiff breeze from the back door, that was still unlatched, made me go all shivery. There were doors everywhere. Doors to wardrobes, lofts and mysterious airing cupboards whose purpose I couldn't comprehend.

I went to shut the gaping back door. Then I

changed my mind. There was something about the air, once you allowed yourself to take it in, that was character forming. Underneath my clothes, I sensed my new character assembling.

My hands felt too big for the teacup Mrs Abbot passed to me. "Drink it," she said, "before it gets cold." Burning my throat, I drank my tea down in three swallows which was much too quick. In order to catch my bus home, I'd have to leave promptly. But my eyelids felt heavy.

Mrs Abbot closed the curtains. In the darkened room, shadows lengthened and moved up to the ceiling, but I didn't move. I could feel my face settle in the firelight. With my hands in my lap, I smoothed the material of my skirt and gazed at my plump arms. I leaned back on the settee. Fire reddened the tips of my shoes. Mrs Abbot leaned her head back too, revealing her false teeth. I was going to miss my bus if I didn't leave now. Resting one arm delicately across the cushions, I felt like I was inside a painting. Head back, chin raised showing the curve of my throat, I fell asleep.

For once, the men I used to know did not intrude on my dreams. Instead a large pale guy, with an angry expression, waved a stick in my face, putting my courage to the test.

About the Writers

David Almond's novels (*Skellig*, *Kit's Wilderness*, *Heaven Eyes* and *Secret Heart*) and his story collection, *Counting Stars* , have established him as one of the finest living children's authors. His many awards include The Carnegie Medal and The Whitebread Prize. His books are translated into over 20 languages, and are being adapted for film, stage and radio. His first story collections (*Sleepless Nights* and *A Kind of Heaven*) were published by IRON Press.

Andrea Badenoch is the author of two gritty, urban crime novels *Mortal* and *Driven*, both from Pan. *Driven* has been optioned for development as a feature film. Her third novel *Blink* is a murder story set in a County Durham pit village in 1962. This has been described as *'shockingly atmospheric and evocative'* and *'hauntingly vivid'*. Andrea has recently completed a novel for children and is currently at work on a book set in Newcastle's west end. She lives in Newcastle upon Tyne.

Leonard Barras has been writing comic prose and verse for more than half a century, infiltrating every field of communication with his coded anarchy. Nobody has heeded him or even heard of him, for which he is everlastingly thankful.

New Fiction from the North

Chaz Brenchley has made a living as a writer since he was eighteen. He has written nine thrillers, most recenty *Shelter*, and a fantasy series, *The Books of Outremer*. He won the 1998 British Fantasy Award and the Northern Writer's Award in 2000. He lives in Newcastle on Tyne with two cats and a famous teddy bear.

Christopher Burns is the author of a collection of short stories and five novels, the most recent of which is *Dust Raising*. Earlier novels have recently been republished in Germany and France. He is one of the new entries in the current Oxford Companion to English Literature. He lives in Cumbria.

Fiona Cooper has written a book of short stories and seven novels, most recently, *Blossom at the Mention of your Name* (Serpent's Tail). She is a spiritualist medium and psychic artist who divides her time between living in Northumberland and working at the residential spiritual awareness centre -Hafan Y Coed in the Brecon Beacons. She is currently working on a book on Soul Therapy. She shares her life with her partner and her dog, Jess, both of whom are angels.

Julia Darling lives and writes in Newcastle. She has written plays, poems, short stories and one novel and is still doing battle with a second. Her first novel, *Crocodile Soup*, was long listed for the Orange Prize, and has recently been published in

Canada, America and Denmark. She is currently a fellow at Newcastle University, a post funded by the Royal Literary Fund.

Chrissie Glazebrook has worked in a zoo, a vegetarian restaurant, and as a radio and television presenter. She was a feature writer for the late *Jackie* magazine and has been published in a range of other magazines and newspapers, including a stint as Jenny Talia, a spoof agony aunt. Her first novel, *The Madolescents*, was published by Heinemann in February 2001.

Wendy Robertson is an ex-teacher, lecturer and journalist and Arts Council Writer-mentor for prisoners in English prisons. She has grown up and worked in the North but always, she avers, with a world outlook. She has published short stories and articles. Her sixteenth novel, *My Dark Eyed Girl* (Headline), set at the time of the Spanish Civil War, came out in September 2000.

Website: www.wendy-robertson.co.uk

Anne Spillard's stories have appeared in publications ranging from *London Magazine* and *Critical Quarterly* to *Penthouse Magazine*. A collection of her stories was published by Hamish Hamilton (1988) and reprinted in Pan Paperbacks in 1989. Her novel, *The Cartomancer* (Hamish Hamilton, 1987, Pan 1989) won the Yorkshire Post Best First Novel Award. Her stories have also been broadcast on BBC Radio. She was born in Leeds and now lives in Cumbria.

New Fiction from the North

Michael Standen, a child of wartime London, has lived half his life in the North(Cumberland, then Durham). His day (and evening)job has been in adult education (the WEA) and publications include four novels with Heinemann and one with OUP. Flambard have published collections of his poetry and short stories.

Margaret Wilkinson is a New Yorker transplanted to the North East of England. Her work has appeared in various literary magazines including *Stand* and *The Printer's Devil*. Her collected stories, *1956*, have recently been published by Diamond Twig. Her first novel, *Ocean Avenue*, was published by Serpent's Tail. Currently, she teaches on the MA in creative writing at The University of Northumbria. The column she writes for the magazine *MsLexia* is called *The Blank Page*.

Kitty Fitzgerald (editor) has published two novels *Marge* (Sheba) and *Snapdragons* (Brandon)and had short stories published in various anthologies, most recently in *Reader I Murdered Him Too* (Women's Press). Four plays have been broadcast on BBC Radio 4 and she wrote the award winning feature film *Dream On* (Amber Films). She has had seven theatre plays produced plus a joint collection of poetry - with Valerie Laws - *For Crying Out Loud* (IRON Press), and has edited several books including *IRON Women* (IRON Press).